MW01126184

IT AIN'T ALWAYS SUNNY ON THE SUNNY SIDE

J.L. FICKLING

Copyright © 2016 J.L. FICKLING

All rights reserved.

ISBN: 1537010417
ISBN-13:978-1537010410

DEDICATION

To Camryn, Kaden and KJ...You are my reason. Everything I do, I do for you. My three chambers: thank you for giving me love, courage and strength beyond what is normal. I love you DEEP.

1

As Sunny lay drowning in her own blood she sees glimpses of her life and wonders, "how did I end up here? God please don't let me die. If you give me one more chance I promise to live my life the way you see fit. Just give me another chance God; I'm not ready to leave my child. Please don't let me leave. I have to make it up to my baby."

✝

Sunny was a typical 8 year old girl. She loved playing with her cabbage patch dolls and the latest Barbie dolls. She was a carefree child and the baby of her family which consisted of her older brother James, Mom Sheila and her Step Dad Samuel. Sunny's parents divorced when she was only 3 years old. When she was 4 her mother moved her and her brother out of Detroit and into a small city called Inkster. She visited her father twice a month. Her visits with her dad were filled with junk food and checking out the latest movies at the theater or going to the park. She really didn't look forward to those visits but she never voiced her feelings on the matter, she went along with the program.

School was out for the summer and Sunny couldn't be more excited. She got to tag-a-long with her brother James wherever he went due to both parents working and him being the oldest.

James dreaded this time, he wanted to do his own thing as most typical 14 year old boys.

 "Sunny sit your ass down somewhere and watch T.V., shit! I'm about to have company and you bet not come downstairs" James said in a scolding irritated tone as he jogged downstairs to his domain. "Ooh I'm telling mama you cursed at me nigga! I don't give a care I don't want to be around you and your funky friends anyway! Shoot...Punky Brewster is about to come on so get out! Ooh I can't stand him; I can't wait for mama to get home. His fat butt is going to get it." Sunny goes to her room and cuts on Punky Brewster. It's a re-run so she starts channel surfing and watches one of her favorite episodes of Charles in Charge. Sunny heard laughing from downstairs and she smelled something funny.

She decided to creep to the bottom of the steps to see just what the heck James was up to. "Ooh you smoking cigarettes!! You are going to get it, I'm telling!!!" James was fuming, "Sunny didn't I tell you not to come down here? Man I swear you are a brat; where are your friends? Oh I forgot you don't have any ah hahaha!!" Sunny's feelings were hurt by her brother's comment; because her friends were at summer camp and she couldn't go this year. James was obviously high as a kite; smoking weed with his friend in his mother's basement. "Aye man chill out she's just a little girl" said Eric, James friend and next door neighbor. Sunny looked at Eric and he gave her a little wink as to say its ok I won't let him hurt you anymore. Sunny felt butterflies in her stomach and she couldn't contain her blushing cheeks and smile so she ran upstairs as fast as she could, jumped in her bed and screamed into her pillow. She always had a crush on Eric but he never acknowledged her until today. She felt as if she was floating and she knew that Eric would be her boyfriend. Why else would he wink at her Sunny thought?

James came upstairs to apologize to his sister after realizing she might really snitch on him. He bribed her by saying he would buy her a screwball ice cream off the ice cream truck the next time it came by. Sunny agreed of course. After that day Eric came over almost every day it seemed to hang out with James and smoke. As usual, James had to bribe Sunny with an ice cream so she wouldn't rat him out.

Sunny ran to the door to beat her brother from answering it first because she wanted to greet Eric. She always won, and when she opened the door every time without fail Eric would gently caress her face and say, "Hey beautiful how's my future girlfriend?" Sunny would giggle and blush and say, "Fine" and she would run back in her room. This particular day Sunny was watching T.V. as usual while her brother entertained his friend. She fell asleep; and Eric asked James to run to the candy store off Carlysle Street to get them some snacks. James was reluctant to go but when Eric pulled out a wad of 5's and 10's from his recently cashed McDonald's check, he threw him 20 bucks and told him to keep the change and didn't have any problems after that.

Once James left, Eric went upstairs to check on Sunny. He watched her as she lay peacefully with ice cream dried up on the corners of her mouth. He smirked. He came inside her room and knelt down beside her. He became aroused. He kissed her on the mouth and she didn't budge. He kissed her again this time trying to insert his tongue; she jumped up and gasped. She was disoriented, confused and still groggy. Eric sat on Sunny's bed and said, "Come here beautiful come sit on my lap." Sunny obliged. She sat on his lap still rubbing the sleep from her eyes. Eric started to rub up and down her back and he slowly moved his hands to her behind and in between her thighs. "What are you doing? Why are you doing that?" Sunny said. Eric replied, "I'm just trying to show you how a boyfriend makes his girlfriend

7

feel special." "You my boyfriend?" said Sunny.

"Only if you want me to be, you are so pretty can I kiss you?" "Umm, where's my brother?" a scared Sunny uttered. "He'll be back soon so we have to hurry. We can't tell him or nobody else that we're boyfriend and girlfriend ok? No one can know because you'll get into a lot of trouble" Eric said sternly.

Sunny was confused and she didn't understand what Eric was doing and why he did it, but her young 8 year old body liked it. She was so confused because she knew what he was doing was wrong but she didn't understand why it felt good. She let Eric kiss her. Eric told her she doesn't know how to kiss so he would teach her. He taught her how to move her tongue in and out his mouth. She was embarrassed but she liked him so much she did what he wanted.

He told her that she has to learn how to kiss his penis too, and she tensed up and became terrified. Eric held her and caressed her head and put her mind at ease by telling her it was ok and she shouldn't be afraid. They were doing what people in love do and if she loved him she would do it. Eric slowly unzipped his pants and pulled his penis out from a slit in his underwear. Sunny had never seen a penis before; she was afraid to look at it. "Give me your hand beautiful. Don't be scared just touch it" Eric said. Sunny did exactly what Eric wanted her to do and she felt a funny feeling in her vagina. She felt funny but in a good way. Her 8 year old mind couldn't understand the magnitude of everything that was taking place. Eric told her to get up because he didn't want her to be scared. He started masturbating in front of her and she became frightened. His face was contorted and his eyes rolled back in his head and he let out a growl.

Sunny ran in the bathroom and shut the door bawling her eyes out as Eric ejaculated in her panties left on the bed. After he composed himself he went in the bathroom and took a wash rag, wet it with warm water and dried her face and told her, "Don't cry pretty girl that's just what a man does when his girlfriend makes him very happy. You make me so happy I exploded with love juice." She didn't know what he was saying; it was as if he was speaking a foreign language. He could sense her confusion and uneasiness so he picked her up and gave her a big hug and told her, "This is our secret o.k.? You can't tell or you will get a whooping by your mom and dad ok?" Sunny said "O.K. I won't tell."

James came in the house with red stained fingers from eating hot cheese doodles and his sister and Eric were downstairs playing duck hunt. James said, "Man why is you playing with my sister dog? Your big 16 year old ass playing duck hunt with my baby sister. Ay Sunny go outside Sara is waiting on you she just got back home." Sunny was tempted to kiss her new boyfriend but he looked at her as if to say you bet not. So she looked at the floor and ran upstairs and straight outside to her best friend Sara.

"Sunny I missed you give me a hug!" The two girls embraced as if they hadn't seen each other in months and it was only 4 weeks. "I got

the new Barbie and Ken motor home you want

me to bring it outside?" said Sara. "Yeah I'll

bring my Barbie's out too!" The girls played with

their Barbie's on the porch and had a good ole

time. Sunny wanted to tell Sara so bad that she

had a boyfriend. It was killing her to hold it in.

She couldn't hold it a minute longer so she told

Sara everything. Sara's parents were very open

with her and they taught her about her body

parts and how sacred they are; and if anyone

touches you in any way, they are wrong no

matter what they say and you should run and

tell an adult. "Sunny he was not supposed to do

that to you! My daddy told me nobody is

supposed to touch you down there. It's a bad

thing and if somebody does that you supposed

to tell on him!" screamed Sara. "No! That's not

true he is my boyfriend and that's what

boyfriend and girlfriend do! And you better not

say nothing to my mama cuz I'm gonna get a

whooping if you do!!" Sunny frantically stated.

"Ooh I shouldn't have told you, you just wish

you had a boyfriend! Your ugly ass! You bet not

say nothing or you will never have a boyfriend!"

Sunny screeched. "Who are you calling ugly

with your big head ass! I'm not even talking to

you no more. Get off my porch! I'm going in the

house you stupid ugly ass! GO HOME!" Sara

said with tears streaming down her face.

Sunny felt her friend was jealous. She

didn't understand what Sara was trying to say

because her parents never talked to her about

things like that; she would hear different things

from school about good and bad touch but it

was never reiterated at home. It didn't resonate with her. At that moment, this is what set the tone for what Sunny would look for in the opposite sex; someone dominating and telling her nothing but what she wanted to hear. No matter how wrong the act was; because she just wanted to feel wanted and loved. Something she didn't feel from her biological father.

As time went on, Sunny started to develop feelings for Eric. He wanted to molest her even further with vaginal penetration. It was nothing short of an act of God because for some reason on this day Sunny was tired of the things Eric did to her. She knew it was wrong and she knew what he wanted to do to her on this day was even more wrong. This was the first time she told Eric no. He didn't like when she rejected him and Sunny saw a side of him she'd

never seen before. He picked her up and

slammed her on his bed and told her to shut the

fuck up. For some reason Sunny felt enraged

and she started bucking like a bull. She went

crazy on him. Sunny scratched him from every

which way she could; she bit, clawed, punched

and slapped until he gave up and left her house

to never return. She was 10 years old. Her

parents never knew their child was being

abused. All the signs were there but they didn't

take heed.

2

Sunny is now 12 years old in the 6th
grade. She has a womanly shape and she's
going through puberty; to say the least she's
"smelling herself." All the boys liked her
because she has light complexion and long hair.
She didn't have an interest in boys yet. It
seems on the surface the abuse she endured
had no lasting effect. She met a boy named Ezra
who really took an interest in her. He told all of
his friends how much he liked her and she was
going to be his girlfriend, she laughed at him

and blew it off. But Ezra was persistent and he finally grew on her. Sunny started to develop feelings for him and she finally accepted his proposal of boyfriend and girlfriend by checking the yes box in the letter he sent her during 5th period.

Ezra would walk Sunny home from school every day and carried her books for her without fail. After 3 weeks, he got up the nerve to ask for a kiss. This was Sunny's first official kiss in her eyes. She told him "yeah you can kiss me", and Ezra closed his eyes and moved slowly towards her mouth and kissed her. But Sunny took over and kissed Ezra the way Eric showed her how. When she finished, Ezra said, "Sunny I love you." "No you don't, you don't even really know me like that Ezra." "I know more than you think! I know what I feel! You don't love me?"

Questioned Ezra. "Yeah I love you too, Ezra.

Do you want to come in my house for a

minute?" Ezra eyes were as big as half dollars.

"Your house?! Ain't your mama home? What if

somebody see I'm in there?" Sunny rolled her

eyes and said, "My mama at work and Samuel is

up North hunting. Come on stop acting like a

chicken shit" Ezra was scared but he wanted to

see if he could make it to second base with

Sunny.

Sunny let Ezra in and asked him if he

wanted something to drink. He kindly asked for

red kool-aid. She made Ezra's drink and led

him to her room. She took off her coat, put her

backpack on the floor and closed her door.

Sunny sat on the bed next to Ezra and asked

him what he wanted to do. "Whatever you want to do. You got some movies or something?" said Ezra. "I don't want to watch movies. I want to have sex, because I love you and you love me."

Ezra choked on his kool-aid and spilled it down his shirt. Sunny snickered and asked if he was alright. He nodded his head yes. Sunny was acting as if she was a 20 year old woman. She sat Ezra's glass of kool-aid on her nightstand and slowly took her shirt off. She turned around and unsnapped her bra and when she turned back around she let her bra fall to the floor.

Ezra was shocked with his mouth hanging wide open. "Suck on my titties Ezra. I want you to suck on my titties nice and slow" Sunny told Ezra. Ezra took a big gulp and took one of Sunny's 12 year old breast in his 13 year old mouth and sucked like he was sucking on a blow pop. Sunny let out a moan as she reached her hands inside of Ezra's pants to feel his 13 year old dick. She immediately snatched her hand out of his pants and yelled, "You nasty nigga! Did you piss on yourself?" "What? Naw I ain't piss on myself! What the fuck is wrong with you! Man, back up off me bro. Put your shit on I'm out!" Ezra left Sunny standing there confused and hurt. "What just happened?" Sunny thought aloud. She didn't know what semen was and never felt nor seen it. Eric would always ejaculate where she couldn't see it and no one talked to her about the particulars of the birds and the bees.

The next day at school Sunny and Ezra avoided each other. They avoided each other the entire school year. In fact, they didn't see each other again until her freshman year of high school. By this time, Sunny dated a few boys but she never went all the way with any of them until Anthony, her current beau. She was still in love with Ezra in her mind and she wanted to wait for him. Even though she hadn't seen Ezra in 3 years, she and Anthony got hot and heavy one too many times and it lead to him popping her cherry.

Ezra was a hooligan. After sixth grade he hung with the wrong crowd, got into drugs and dropped out of school. He started to sell drugs for his crew; the *"garden block",* which is a reference to the people who live in one of the two housing projects in Inkster called Le Moyne Gardens. Ezra thought he was the man around town and Sunny never left his thoughts. By this time, Ezra had sex with quite a few girls and was well experienced at his young age. But, Sunny never left his mind nor heart.

Ezra finally built up the nerve to go up to Sunny's school and wait for her to come out after school was dismissed. The school bell rung, and 15 minutes later there was his Sunny. Now, 14 years old and built like a twenty year old. She was thick in all the right places. Some would call her chubby for her age but not Ezra. She was just right to him with long black hair flowing down her back. She had a glow about her. Ezra's dick instantly got hard but, it was more than physical for him. He felt a tug at his heart along with his dick. Sunny didn't see Ezra she was too busy gossiping with her girlfriend Tyra. As she walked past Ezra he quickly grabbed her hand and she looked back at Ezra and dropped her books. Ezra said, "Why you don't call me no mo?" and gave her a wink.

Sunny snatched her hand back and said, "Uh, Do I know you?" with a devilish grin on her face.

"Oh you gone play me like that huh?" Ezra reached over to Sunny and grabbed her face firmly but not rough and tongued her down. The kids at school started hooting and hollering.

Sunny's panties were instantly soaking wet but after about 5 seconds of the kiss she pushed him off of her and said, "Nigga I don't know where your mouth been you got me fucked up! And besides I don't think my man would appreciate you tonguing his girl down" Tyra was cracking up the entire time because she knew Sunny's true feelings were for Ezra. "I could give a fuck less about your hoe ass man. He ain't got shit to do with me but, you do. So, you cheating on me now?" Ezra said in a serious tone. "You sound crazy as hell. You better go before he comes out" Sunny said sarcastically. Ezra looked at her and said, "Alright I'll catch you when you're alone. I see you like to show out in front of your friends but you remember you gon be my girl" if Sunny was a popsicle she would've melted all over the sidewalk but she tried to keep her cool and play hard to get. "Whatever Nigga" as she grinned and rolled her eyes only to find her 11th grade, 200 lbs, 6' boyfriend standing in front of her. "Who the fuck is this clown, Sunny?" Anthony growled. "Oh he's an old friend from elementary he..." before Sunny could finish Ezra interrupted "Oh what up play boy I'm Ezra. Sunny used to be my lil honey back in the day and I just wanted to say what

up, it's all good" "So what the fuck you kissing

on my girl for Nigga?" said Anthony in a low but

serious tone. Sunny got in front of Anthony and

said, "You need to stop tripping for real, let's just

go. Come walk me home" by this time Ezra's

friends were surrounding him telling him to drop

Anthony. Anthony didn't care; he felt like he

had to claim his territory so, he tongued Sunny

down and said "this is my girl Nigga don't get it

twisted!" Sunny felt like vomiting at that

moment. Her feelings for Anthony vanished at

that moment. He disgusted her.

Ezra said, "You disrespect my girl like that

again muthafucka you gon regret yo daddy ever

fucked yo mama and had your gumpy looking

ass" Anthony swung on Ezra but missed his

face completely and hit his arm. Anthony is about 30 lbs. heavier and 4 inches taller so no one understood how Anthony could miss his face. All Ezra could do was laugh and proceed to stomp a mud hole in Anthony. Tyra pulled Sunny away practically dragging her, "Sunny come the fuck on before the po po's come up here! You know these garden block fools gon get to shooting! Come on bitch, shit!" Sunny snapped out of her trance and ran with Tyra back to her house. "Girl did you see my baby oh my goodness I can't believe his crazy ass beat up Anthony over me." Sunny said in a high pitched squealing voice. "Yeah I saw that shit alright. That nigga crazy, you don't need to get back with him. He ain't nothing but a hood nigga" said Tyra unimpressed. "You know I got a weakness for bad boys so, talk to the hand" Sunny said jokingly, but she wasn't joking. She had a weakness for rough necks.

After talking about the day's event and going over homework Tyra went home. It was about 9:00pm and the phone rang. Sunny picked it up on the third ring after no one else bothered to answer. "Hello" said Sunny irritated. "Come outside in about 15 minutes I'm about to walk over" said Ezra. "Ok girl I'll bring it to you" said Sunny as she picked up the phone. "Who was that?" questioned Sunny's mother. "Just Tyra she forgot her calculator. I'm about to go take it to her" "Uh did you ask me if you could take it to her?" Sunny's mother said in an authoritative tone. Sunny smacks her lips and says, "I'm just taking her calculator to her what's the big deal?" "You know what, you take it to her when you see her in school with your

smart ass mouth. Get your ass in that kitchen

and finish them got damn dishes like I told you

to do earlier when I was at work with your fast

ass! You think somebody stupid? You better

cool your hot ass off before I do it for you; and

trust me you won't like it heifer" Sunny knew

not to say another word after her mother scolded

her. All Sunny could do is cry because she

thought Ezra would think she didn't want

anything to do with him by not coming outside

like he asked. She was crying uncontrollably.

Her mother thought she was crazy and

hormonal so she told her to go to bed.

Sunny decided to take a shower before she

went to bed, but she couldn't get Ezra off her

mind. She was so hot and wet at the mere

thought of him. As the shower beat against her body she felt an outer body experience. She felt hands all over her as she daydreamed it was Ezra's hand. She started to pleasure herself. Encircling her clitoral pearl: feeling it pulsate, growing bigger and harder. She had to grab her wash cloth and bite down on it to muffle her moans. Finally after 5 minutes of stimulation, she climaxed so hard she collapsed to the shower floor. It was so intense for Sunny; she never masturbated before. Her step father and mother bust into the bathroom thinking she'd hurt herself. She tried to play it off like she slipped. She couldn't do anything but burst into a laughing fit while slipping into her pj's. "Ezra baby please don't give up on me yet" Sunny said to herself as she drifted off to sleep.

Sunny heard Ezra got locked up the next day at school. Anthony's parents pressed charges. She was heartbroken. She had to run into the bathroom at school and cry her heart out. She faked a stomach ache and went home for the day and cried all day and night. She didn't know what to do. Ezra wouldn't be released until he was 18. Sunny eventually snapped out of her depression and dated other boys in high school. None could compare to Ezra in her eyes but she went along with it until she was bored and moved onto the next guy. She was sexually active and none of her boyfriends could make her climax. She would have to finish the job herself whenever she was alone. She didn't feel a connection with anyone the way she did with Ezra.

3

It's the summer of 99'. Sunny and her friends have graduated and are enjoying the summer before everyone leaves for college the end of august. Sunny's cell phone went off it was her friend Shalisha. "What up hoochie what's the deal?" Sunny said jokingly. "Shut up trick! Look it's a party at the Warehouse Downtown you want to go?" asked Shalisha. "Do I want to go? Bitch, please you know you didn't have to ask that; hell yeah! Let me see if I can get my mama's car cause I ain't trying to be downtown in your hoopty ass festiva" "fuck you Sunny with your hook head ass. That's cool let me know what she say" Shalisha hung up the phone. Sunny's Mom was proud of her accomplishments with school and more importantly she graduated without a baby on her hip; she pretty much let Sunny do whatever. She was a good kid.

Sunny pulled up at Shalisha's to pick her up for the club. She honks her horn, "beep beep beep. This tramp always late, shit" Sunny said irritated. Shalisha was about 5'4" dark brown complexion with a killer ass body and a big booty. She wore a long weave but it fit her and her personality. She kept her nails and toes done. Her nails had to be about 2" long. She was ghetto fabulous but a cutie none the less.

Shalisha comes running out the house with a black mini skirt on; showing the bottom of her ass cheeks and a silver halter top with silver strappy 4" heel sandals. She was looking good; slutty, but good. "Damn you gone wake the neighbors! You know I'm slow" Shalisha said jokingly. "Yeah, short bus slow" Sunny said laughing. "So who gon be at the Warehouse you think? It should be a nice turnout the Warehouse is always jumping on a Friday" Said Sunny. "I don't know but some niggas is throwing a coming home party for some nigga named Ezra" Sunny almost crashed her mom's car. "Bitch what the fuck is wrong with your crazy ass??" Shalisha screamed. "Did you say Ezra?" Sunny asked. "Yeah! why you know him or something?" "Yeah something like that"

exclaimed Sunny. She could hardly contain
herself. She had to put on some Busta Rhymes
to drown out her anxiousness over seeing Ezra
tonight.

Sunny and Shalisha got to the club
around 1130pm. The line was wrapped around
the building. As soon as they got out the car the
hounds were on them with cat calls, whistles
and got damns. Sunny slimmed down a bit but
not too much. She was a perfect size 10 with a
lots of tits and a nice round ass; not too big
though. Nowhere near Shalisha's size. Sunny
had on a mini Tommy Hilfiger jean skirt, a
bright pink shiny halter top with a pair of bright
pink strappy heel sandals. Her tattoos on her
back and arm were blazing making her look
more seductive. The two ladies looked at the

line and said "Fuck that" in unison and trotted

to the front, flirted with the bouncers and got in

with ease. The club was jumping and Sunny was

scoping the place for Ezra but she didn't see

him. She tried to take her mind off of it by

hitting the blunt in the bathroom with Shalisha

and that did the trick. She was loose and feeling

good, she was ready to dance. She and Shalisha

went out on the dance floor. The guys were all

over them and they loved it. Sunny felt someone

smack her on the ass. She spun around fast to

see who: it was Ezra.

She couldn't do anything but smile. He

pulled her close to him and gave her a tight hug;

he didn't want to let her go. He had to yell in

her ear, "I'm not letting you go this time" Ezra

grabbed her hand and they went on the stage

dancing and grinding on each other. He had a liter of gin in his hand and a blunt in his mouth with his homeboys surrounding him chanting, "My nigga's home, My nigga's home" It was 2:30am and the party was still going strong.

The DJ announced that the party wasn't over until 3 in the morning; everybody went wild.

Shalisha found Sunny and reminded her, "Bitch, you got your mama shit out this late she's going to get in that ass!" Sunny forgot all about driving her mom's car. She went to Ezra and asked him to step outside with her.

Shalisha came along she figured the night was over and it was time to go home. "I got to go home. I got my mom's car so you know how that go, but I want your number" Sunny told Ezra. "Why don't I just follow you and you drop the car off and come back with me?" Ezra told

Sunny. "That'll work" Sunny said with a coy look on her face.

On the ride home Sunny told Shalisha the scoop on she and Ezra. "Girl you are gone fuck him tonight! You slut. I want to know all the details you hear me?" Shalisha yelled. "You tripping! I ain't fucking tonight. I just want to chill with him" Sunny stated matter of factly. "Bitch, who you think you fooling? Your pussy probably soaking wet right now and he just got out of the joint too? Oh yeah, ain't nothing like that good ole tight 18 year old wet pussy. He prolly can smell your wet ass all the way in his car, hahahahaa!" "Get out the car Shalisha. I can't stand your ass" Sunny stated embarrassed. "Bye slut! Don't forget safe sex or no sex" Shalisha closed the door and went inside her home. Sunny drove her Moms car home and went inside. She put the keys on the kitchen counter and tried to sneak back out.

"Uh, where are you going?" Sunny's mom asked. "I'm spending the night over Shalisha's Ma." "MmmHmm alright bye" "Thanks for letting me use your car mom I'll see ya tomorrow!" Sunny couldn't wait to get out that house and thank God Ezra had enough sense to cut his music down while waiting for Sunny.

"So where are we going Mr. Ezra Carmichael?" Sunny asked. "Back to my hotel room to chill and catch up if that's alright with you baby girl?" Sunny's pussy jumped at the mere thought of finally getting to make love to the man she's been in love with for the past six years. "That's cool" Sunny said nonchalantly.

On the car ride, the two talked about his stint in Juvenile Detention and how it was hard on him but he got through it and he wouldn't take back what he did. They held hands and she told him about her going away to Spellman University in a few weeks. Ezra told her how proud he was of her; but, he had a sad look in his eyes.

They finally got to his hotel. Ezra had a suite at the Pontchartrain Hotel. It was decked out with a bar, Jacuzzi you name it this room had it. Sunny was impressed; she'd never been in a hotel quite like this before. She made herself comfortable, took her shoes off and went on the balcony to look at the view of Downtown Detroit. Ezra came up behind her and put his arms around her. He slowly turned her towards him. "I've never loved a woman the way I love you. I have thought about you every day of my life since I met you when we were 13 years old. Not a day has gone by that I haven't thought about you. When I was locked up; I prayed to God that if/when I got out and you were still around Inkster, I would never fuck up and I would make you my wife and leave this street shit behind. I loved you Sunny back then. I love you right now and I will love you until I take my last breath and leave this world" Ezra declared his love for Sunny and a single tear fell from her eye. She grabbed his face gently and pulled him to her. She kissed him so passionately. They kissed for what seemed like an eternity until Ezra stepped back and picked Sunny up as she straddled him with her legs wrapped around his waist. He laid her on the bed and undressed her slowly. "I've been dreaming about this moment for a long muthafuckin time baby. I want to take my time and do it right" Sunny didn't utter a word. Ezra took every stitch of clothing off of Sunny as she lay in the bed and he just stood back and admired her beauty and her body. He thought she looked so angelic. He wanted to taste and touch every inch of her body.

Ezra guided Sunny to get up and follow him into the bathroom. The shower was a standup shower; he turned it on and took off all of his clothes. They both stared at each other in awe. Ezra grabbed Sunny's hand and led her in the shower. He washed her from head to toe and she did the same for him. He put the hotel robe on her and he did the same for himself. He gently dried her off and put lotion all over her body. Sunny returned the favor but she couldn't wait any longer; she needed wanted desired his dick in her mouth. She turned him over and his dick was rock hard. Sunny, slowly swirled her tongue around the head of his big, black, thick dick. Ezra moaned in ecstasy. Sunny then licked up and down the shaft of his dick like it was a chocolate dicksicle. Ezra could hardly contain himself. He was about to explode.

Sunny felt his dick pulsating. She then took as much of his dick inside of her mouth and down her throat that would fit. Slowly but steady in a rhythmic motion; she bobbed up and down on his dick until his seeds exploded down her throat. Ezra was trembling. Sunny slowly and gently took his dick out of her mouth and said, "I love you Ezra Carmichael." Ezra got up and kissed the love of his life. He motioned for her to

lie down. He started kissing her neck and slowly

traced her body with his tongue all the way

down to her toes. Sunny was so turned on she

climaxed and Ezra hadn't touched her pussy yet.

He finally got to her creamy center and gently

pushed her legs behind her head to see her

wetness gush down the crack of her ass. Ezra

was instantly brick hard again. "I've been dying

to taste you baby" Ezra gently opened the lips of

Sunny's prize. He softly licked her pussy lips

then her supple pussy walls and finally her clit.

He buried his face inside of her wetness and

refused to come up for air. Sunny burst into the

most intense orgasm she's ever experienced in

all her life. It was so intense Ezra came at the

same time as she. When the spasms stopped,

Ezra took his hard black cock and gently rubbed

up and down Sunny's pussy causing her to moan and clench up with anticipation of his dick entering her. Ezra gently entered her pussy. It was so warm, wet and tight he could barely contain himself. He slowly and steady eased his 8.5" dick inside Sunny's tight 18 year old pussy. Sunny winced in pain and pleasure. Ezra took it slow and easy at first; and then he started gaining momentum. His thrust became deeper and stronger. He looked at her intently in her eyes. They never stopped looking at each other. Not once. "I....Love...You Sunny" Ezra panted. Sunny couldn't utter a word she was in a state of pure bliss and ecstasy. She was in a trance. Sunny never experienced love making like this. Ezra dick was pounding on Sunny's pussy. She wanted to climb up the walls but Ezra had her by her waist so she couldn't go anywhere. They both went to a place of pure

pleasure and they both climaxed as one:

Screaming, shaking, moaning, they couldn't

contain themselves. It was as if their bodies

fused together and they became one.

4

After that night Ezra and Sunny became inseparable. They spent every waking hour together for the next two weeks until it was time for Sunny to leave for Spellman. She didn't bring up the fact of her leaving until the day before her departure. She wanted Ezra to come down south with her. She didn't know how, but she wanted to make a way. "Ezra, you know I leave tomorrow and I can't be without you. I want you to come down there. Maybe you can save up some money and find us a place; that way I can live off campus and you could even get a job. It's all kinds of opportunities for young black men in Atlanta. What do you think?" Ezra looked at Sunny for what seemed forever and his face began to change into a look of disgust. "You sound crazy as hell. You think I'm gone leave my family and friends to chase after your ass? I don't fucking think so. I mean it was just sex, right? Shit, we only spent a few days together. The pussy was good but it wasn't that good. I'll get wit you. Gone and do the college girl thang, I'll holla" Ezra got up from the couch at Sunny's mom house and started walking towards the stairs to leave. Sunny was stunned and in a state of shock. She jumped up from the couch, pulled Ezra's arm and pushed him with both hands in his chest and said, "What the fuck did you just say to me? You just wanted some pussy and that's it? Huh? Are

you serious right now E?" Sunny was so angry

tears were streaming down her face but her

voice didn't crack. She was trembling from head

to toe. She could feel her heart break and her

blood started to boil. "I mean, yeah. Shit you

was a hoe when we was kids and you a hoe now.

What did you expect? Now back the fuck up I'm

about to bounce!"

It was killing Ezra to talk this way to

Sunny, but he felt as if she was rejecting him.

He didn't want her to leave him. He didn't know

how to express his true feelings so he decides to

cope with his pain by causing Sunny pain. Hurt

people, hurt people. It took every ounce of

strength in his body not to break down and cry

but he felt crying is for bitches; real men don't

cry. Sunny became enraged and started to attack Ezra. She punched, kicked and scratched Ezra all the while screaming, "I hate your muthafucking ass! I hate you! I hope you die you piece of shit! I fucking hate you!" Ezra finally got a good hold of Sunny and pinned her to the ground and started to choke her. "You stupid bitch! Who the fuck you think you fucking with huh?! I should kill yo hoe ass bitch! I should kill you since you want to leave me! Yeah, that's right bitch! You trying to leave me to fuck the next nigga, huh bitch? Can't nobody have you if I can't! I mean that shit!" Ezra said yelling at the top of his lungs and crying. If Sunny's parents were at home Ezra would've ended up back in jail for what he was doing to Sunny.

Sunny was gasping for air and she felt faint. She was about to pass out until Ezra's face soften and he let her go and collapsed right next to her on the floor. He was out of breath and crying inconsolably. Sunny was gagging and coughing; searching for oxygen. She found the strength to crawl to the sink attached to the washer. She turned on the water and tried to sip from the faucet. She immediately vomited in the sick and fell back to her knees crying. But, she wasn't crying because of what Ezra did to her. She was crying for Ezra. She felt terrible about what he was feeling. She felt it was her fault. She couldn't leave him. She wouldn't be able to live with herself. She never felt love like this for any man and she felt that no man has ever loved her as deeply as Ezra. She finally got the strength to walk over to Ezra who was sitting on the floor with his back against the couch and tears streaming down his face, but no sound came from him. Sunny knelt down and said, "I'm sorry E. I didn't know you felt this way. I love you baby and I would never leave you. I can go to school here, fuck it. I can't leave you. I just got you back in my life and I'm not trying to lose you. I love you more than life itself" Sunny caressed Ezra's face while talking to him.

Ezra looked at Sunny and felt relief and shame. He never thought he would lose control on Sunny. "I just can't lose you Sunny. I need you. I need you. I'm sorry I lost my temper I just didn't know what else to do. I won't do that shit again, just don't leave me. My heart can't take that shit, Sun." The two embraced each other and made passionate love right there on the basement floor. The love making they shared was so intense; it was as if their hearts shared the same beat. They truly felt a connection like never before.

In the coming weeks Sunny applied to a couple of local Universities and was accepted to Wayne State University. Sunny's parents completely disapproved of her decision to stay in state and refused to help her out financially for choosing to lose her scholarship to Spellman and stay home to be with a hoodlum like Ezra. It was tough on Sunny but she was considered an adult now and she had to follow her heart despite what anyone had to say.

Things were going smoothly between Sunny and Ezra; they were closer than ever. Sunny shared all her skeletons with Ezra and she felt he never judged her. She even told him about her being molested as a child and why she reacted the way she did with their first sexual experience at the age of 12. "If I ever see that muthafucka you best believe I'm killing that nigga!" Ezra told Sunny. "Don't go there. I mean it was in the past I've moved on from it. It's not a big deal and I know what goes around comes around so just leave it alone. Besides, I didn't tell you that so you can get mad and want to kill somebody. I just wanted you to know more about me and what I've been through. You know?" "Yeah alright I respect that baby" Ezra said unconvincingly.

Sunny couldn't be more happy. She was going to school full time, and she was madly in love with the man of her dreams. She became withdrawn from her friends because anytime away from school was spent with her man. She didn't really think too much about it until she got a call from her best friend Tyra. "Hello" Sunny said answering her home phone. "Hey Sun what's up girl? How come I haven't heard from you? What have you been up to?" Tyra said practically yelling at Sunny. "Girl I missed your black ass! I've been so busy with school and E I just forgot about everything else I'm sorry. Will you forgive me?" "Mmm-Hmm, yeah you been busy alright; on them knees! Get that niggas balls out your mouth and come hang with your girl! Eastern is having a party tonight; sort of like the icebreaker. So, you should come hang with your girl!" "Girl, that sounds like a plan. I need to get out after taking all these damn exams this week. Ok tell you what; I'll come to your dorm room around 9:00. Is that cool?" Sunny excitedly asked. She really did miss her friends. "Yeah that's cool I can't wait to see you girl, peace out!" They both hung up the phone.

Sunny immediately heads to her closet to pick out a banging outfit. She put together some skin tight guess jeans with a bustier and 4" heels. "E, loves these damn shoes. O shit I didn't call him and tell him what's up for the night. Let me call and see what he's doing" Sunny calls Ezra but she doesn't get an answer. She even sent him a page but no response. She figured she would stop by his house before she went to Eastern. Sunny pulls up to his Grandmother's house and sees his truck. She rings the doorbell and it's no answer. Sunny thought that was strange. She tried the door and it was unlocked so she helped herself in. Ezra's grandmother was fast asleep on the couch. Sunny didn't want to disturb her so she tiptoed downstairs to Ezra's room. It was dark but he had on his red light. "What the hell is he doing down here? Probably getting high" Sunny thought to herself. She sees Ezra on the couch with his head back eyes closed and blunt in hand. She tiptoes over to him from behind and whispers in his ear, "Boo!"

5

"What the fuck?" Ezra yelled. Ezra's pants were down around his ankles and Sunny's friend Shalisha, was on her knees with Ezra's dick in her mouth. Sunny instantly became enraged. She couldn't speak. All she could do was leap over the couch, grab Shalisha by her throat and bang her head against the concrete basement floor. Shalisha was screaming for her life. "Sunny, baby stop! You gone kill that girl baby stop!!" Ezra screamed while trying to pry Sunny off of Shalisha. Ezra was successful in getting Sunny off of Shalisha . "Shalisha get your rat ass the fuck out my house bitch! Go before she kills your hoe ass!" Shalisha grabbed her shirt and purse and ran up the stairs and out the door with her bare titties bouncing in the wind.

"Ezra! Ezra! What in God's green earth is going on down there boy?" Ezra's grandmother yelled. "Nothing granny go in your room I'm handling some business!" Ezra yelled disrespectfully to his grandmother while holding Sunny by her waist with one arm, and holding her mouth closed with his other hand as she bucks like a wild horse. "Calm down baby please! I'm not going to let you go until you calm down!" Sunny began to calm down. She was breathing heavily; she stopped kicking and swinging her arms. Ezra let her go and Sunny slowly turned around and caught Ezra on his nose, causing blood to squirt out all over his shirt. "You bastard!" Ezra fell to his knees and Sunny kicked Ezra in his nuts. She ran upstairs crying hysterically; she was a wreck. She had no clue how she made it to her best friend's dorm room but as soon as Tyra opened the door she collapsed in her arms. "Sunny, what's wrong baby?" Tyra said concerned and almost frantic.

"Ezra fucked Shalisha! I walked in on her sucking his dick! I'm going to kill that bitch!" Sunny was shaking and sobbing. She was sick to her stomach so she asked for a trash can. She thought she was going to vomit but didn't. Tyra made Sunny lie down with a cold compress on her head. She decided to call Shalisha as she stepped out into the hallway, so that Sunny couldn't hear the conversation. Shalisha picked up the phone on the fourth ring and said a faint hello. "You two time conniving bitch! How could you do that shit to Sunny? We been friends since elementary you trifling hoe. I knew you were a rat but, not a gutter rat! Don't you ever call me again, and if Sunny sees you God help you!" Tyra mashed the off button on her cordless phone. She felt so bad for her friend. She felt as if it had been her that was betrayed: that's how close the two were. Tyra tiptoed back in her room and laid in the bed with her best friend. Sunny stopped crying by this time and she stared at the ceiling. "T, I really thought he would never do any shit like this to me. I never loved anybody the way I love him. I don't understand why. I just want somebody to love me T. That's all I want... That's all I ever wanted since I've been a little girl. I fucking hate him for doing this to me" Sunny started to cry again.

Tyra felt her friends' pain and she wanted to take it away. She kissed Sunny on the forehead and told her it would be ok and she would always be there for her. Sunny turned to Tyra and hugged her tight; she didn't want to let go. Tyra lifted Sunny's chin and looked her in her eyes. She slowly moved towards her lips and kissed her. Sunny kissed her back. Tyra wiped Sunny's tears with her hand and kissed her on the lips again: This time was more sensual, more sexual. The two friends started kissing more passionately and vigorously. "I just want to make you feel better Sunny. Just relax

honey" Tyra whispered. Tyra got up and locked
her door and the bathroom door to the bathroom
she shared with her dorm mates next door. She
got back in bed with Sunny, unbuttoned her
jeans, and slid them off her legs. Sunny's eyes
were swollen and puffy from crying. She
couldn't think straight but she didn't want to
stop her friend. It felt right at the time. Tyra
slowly slid off Sunny's panties and dropped
them on the floor. No words were exchanged by
the friend's, just intense stares. Tyra gently
massaged Sunny's clit as Sunny let out a low
moan. As Tyra continued to massage her best
friend's clit, her hand became wet with Sunny's
juices. Tyra couldn't help herself; she had to
know what her friend tasted like. She buried
her face in Sunny's pussy; and licked and kissed
her clit until she climaxed twice.

As Tyra came up for air her chin was soaked with her best friends juices. "I always wanted to do that" Tyra said as she kissed Sunny's inner thigh. Sunny let out a loud laugh, "Girl what the fuck just happened ha ha ha! What did we do and when did you start licking pussy and why are you this good?" Sunny said, laughing and playing in her friend's hair. Tyra laughed too, "You are the first! I don't know why it just felt right shit, ha ha ha. You know I love your ass so don't trip and don't get it twisted; I still love the dick ha ha ha!" Sunny said while laughing and talking at the same time. The two friends gave each other high fives and kissed on the lips. "I need to take a shower and you need to wash your face you little freak. I do feel a little better though. I love you T come here." The two best friends embraced for what seemed an eternity. That experience they shared changed the dynamics of their friendship forever.

Sunny took a shower at her friend's dorm room and put her clothes back on. She was still hurting, but she tried to mask it. She wanted to party and take her mind off of her pain. She and Tyra were dressed to kill and ready to party. They arrived at the College party a little before midnight. Sunny had 15 messages from Ezra but she refused to talk to him right now. She was on some revenge shit and she needed to numb her pain. Sunny and Tyra smoked a fat L in the ladies' bathroom and drunk a pint of Hennessy each. They were completely wasted. Exactly what Sunny wanted. A senior at the College party took an interest in Sunny. His name was Sabastian. He was 6'4" 240lbs, hazel eyes with caramel complexion and the whitest teeth she'd ever seen. She usually doesn't go for the brothers with light complexion, but he was fine.

"How you doing Ma? You go to school here?" Sabastian yelled in Sunny's ear over the music as they slowed their dancing down. "No I don't and did you know you were fine!" A drunken Sunny slurred. "Yeah I did ha ha ha... so you got a man?" Sabastian inquired with one eyebrow raised biting his lower lip trying to seduce Sunny. It was working. "Yeah I do, but he let my best friend suck his dick today so I'm not really feeling him right now. Do you want to fuck?" Sabastian thought he would choke on his spit. He'd never encountered such an aggressive straight forward girl. "Um, how about we go to

my apartment off campus and blow one?"

"That's cool, but I got to tell my girl first I don't

want her to be worried" Sunny stumbles around

to find Tyra. She spots her getting felt up by

some random dude. "Tyra.....Tyra!!! Excuse me

can you remove your hand from my girl's pussy!

I might need that tonight and I don't want to be

tasting your damn fingers down there, shit!"

Sunny slurred. "Sunny, what the fuck girl!

You're drunk and you know you can't hold your

damn liquor!" Tyra said unable to control her

laughter. "Man whatever, look I'm about to go to

this nigga apartment and blow one; and

hopefully get my pussy ate. So I just wanted to

let you know where I was going. You want to roll

and get in on the action?" "Sunny what the

fuck? You don't even know him?! I'm not letting

you go nowhere, especially not alone. You're just hurting right now baby. Don't do nothing you gon regret." Tyra said being concerned. "Look T I'm grown and I want some dick. And I don't want it from my man so I'm going to get it from pretty boy. If you want you can come too. I don't give a fuck. I really don't; so what's it gone be?" Tyra knew she couldn't let her friend go out like that; and plus, she secretly wanted to get down with her best friend again. "Fuck it, I'm going with you to keep an eye on your ass shit"

Sunny rode with Sebastian and Tyra trailed them in her car. Once in his apartment the girls took a seat on the couch and Sebastian rolled a blunt. "So Sunny, you still down with what you say you wanted to do at the party?" Chuckled Sabastian but he was very serious. "I said it didn't I? Look Sebastian I'm gone be honest. I just want some dick right now; I need it inside me because I'm really fucked up. I just want to get the shit fucked out of me and I want my girl to be here with me, too." Sunny turns to Tyra, "You don't have to fuck Tyra I just want you here with me, ok?" Sunny pleaded. Tyra looked at her tortured friend and she felt bad for her, "I'm here for you Sun, I just don't think..." "Shhh!! please just shut the fuck up and don't tell me what you think is right; cause I don't give a fuck right now Tyra I need this ok?" Sunny interrupted her friend. "Fine" Said Tyra.

Sebastian finished rolling the blunt and they all smoked it until they got to the tail. They were really buzzed and feeling good. Sunny got up straddled Sebastian and started tongue kissing him. Sebastian has been rock hard since they got inside his apartment. He rubbed on Sunny's ass and motioned for Tyra to come and sit next to them. Tyra was soaking wet just from the anticipation of what may happen next. "Tell me what you want me to do daddy." Sunny said to Sebastian. "I want to see you lick her pussy while I fuck you from the back." Sebastian demanded. "Come here Tyra. Come here I owe you one anyway" Sunny said seductively. Sunny undressed herself and Tyra in 10 seconds flat. And before you knew it she was lapping up Tyra's pussy juices with her tongue as Sebastian fucked her doggy style. Sunny heard her cell phone going off in her purse right next to them on the floor. She hoped it was Ezra. She came up for air from eating her best friend pussy and grabbed her phone out of her purse; and sure enough it was Ezra. Sunny pushed the talk

button, "Hey baby what chu doing?" Sunny said

with a slight moan in her voice as she talked.

Sebastian didn't miss a stroke. "Sunny, what

the fuck?! Where are you? I've been calling you.

I went everywhere looking for you babe. I'm

sorry; where are you I need to talk to you." Ezra

pleaded. "Baby I'm getting fucked right now and

I'm eating my girl's pussy so, can it wait?" "You

what? What the fuck you just say?" Ezra yelled.

"Sebastian baby say something?" Sunny said.

"This is some good ass pussy argggh!!" Sebastian

busts a nut in mid-sentence. "See baby, you

didn't have to fuck around on me. Sebastian

said my pussy is the best. I'll get wit you, ok?"

Sunny said with a smirk on her face. "Oh wait

best friend say hi to E?" Tyra laughed

uncontrollably. "Sunny, when I see you bitch,

when I see you I'm gone beat the breaks off your muthafucking ass you nasty ass rat bitch!" **End call.** Sunny felt relieved. She caused him as much pain as he caused her. It still didn't change the fact she loved this man and he betrayed her. She felt sick and ran to Sebastian's bathroom. She vomited for the next 10 minutes and passed out on the floor.

Tyra washed her up as best as she could and Sebastian carried her to Tyra's car and followed them back to her dorm. He was a gentleman and cared about their well-being which was rare especially with the circumstances being the way they were. Sebastian carried Sunny up to Tyra's room and said goodnight. The next morning Sunny felt like shit. Her stomach ached and so did her pussy. All she wanted to do was go home, take a shower and sleep for three days. "Tyra...Tyra wake up. I'm going home honey ok?" Sunny said to her friend. "Alright, you straight?" "Yeah I'm good to go I'll call you." "Love you honey." Tyra said to her friend. "Love you too" It seemed like an 8 hour ride home. Sunny's mind was racing with a million and one thoughts. She didn't know what she was going to do about Ezra. She turned down her street and Ezra's car was parked in front of her parent's house. Fear came over her body like a ton of bricks. Ezra got out of his car and stood next to it waiting for Sunny to pull into the driveway.

Sunny tried to ignore him but he came down on her like a hawk. He grabbed her arm and said, "You shut the fuck up. I don't want you to say shit, you coming with me. If you scream I will break your fucking arm and put two in your head bitch." Sunny didn't say a word she did what Ezra told her to do. Ezra opened the passenger door and put Sunny inside. He strapped her seatbelt for her and closed the door. Ezra got in the driver seat and took off. As soon as he got off her street he yanked on Sunny's seatbelt and wrapped it around her neck trying to choke the life out of her. "You trifling bitch! All I did was get my dick sucked, but you...You eating pussy and fucking random niggas, huh bitch? HUH?! I'll kill both of us in this muthafucka cuz I don't give a fuck!" All Sunny could do was try to get the seatbelt away from her neck but she was unsuccessful. Ezra had the grip too tight. She gasped for air and passed out.

Sunny came to and she realized she was at Ezra's friend house in the basement with her hands tied lying on a cot. She was too afraid to scream so she just laid there and cried. She didn't know Ezra was watching her the entire time. He finally turned on the light and knelt down beside her looking into her eyes intently. "Don't cry now. You know you fucked up don't you?" Whispered Ezra, into Sunny's ear. "E I know I fucked up. I was so fucking hurt and sick from what you did to me I wanted to hurt you back E. It didn't mean shit, it was nothing. I need you baby please don't leave me E, I need you!" Sunny was sobbing uncontrollably; struggling to get her words out. Ezra started to calm down and think more clearly. The cloud of rage started to lift from his head and he felt sorry for what he was doing to the love of his life.

The only woman he ever cared about. "Sunny

we both fucked up, but you took it to a whole

new level. I can't trust you no more Sunny. I --"

"No, shut up! Shut the fuck up don't say that

shit to me!" Sunny interrupted Ezra. "It's me

baby, It's me! You know you can trust me; I was

just on some revenge bullshit. I should've just

stayed and talked it out with you baby. Please

don't leave me!"

Ezra cut the zip tie around his girlfriend's

wrist and set her free. "I ain't going no where

Sun stop crying aight? Stop crying baby come

here" Sunny struggled to get up still feeling

woozy. Ezra took notice and helped her up.

Ezra grabbed Sunny's face and kissed her over

and over again. He felt terrible for what he put

his girlfriend through, but he felt it was justified

in his mind for what she did in return. "How we gon fix this Sun? How can we fix this shit? Shit is all fucked up!" "I'll do whatever it takes E. I don't care whatever you want me to do I'll do it" Sunny said trying to convince him of her loyalty. "First, I want you to suck my dick" Sunny gave Ezra a confused look. "What? Why? Ezra I'm not in the mood for sex." "Oh so you not in the mood now? But you got your pussy banged all night last night and now you not in the mood? This is the shit I'm talking about right here. When a bitch say she not in the mood you know she fucking around. Get the fuck out and walk your ass home. I'm straight on you" Sunny was confused and heartbroken. She felt dirty and used. A feeling she knew all too well. A feeling she hasn't felt since she was molested.

She tried to snap out of it. She couldn't lose her man; he was all she wanted and all she really knew. Nobody in this world could make her feel the way he made her feel. Sunny started to unzip Ezra pants. "I said I'll do whatever it takes E and I mean that shit" Sunny said with a cocky attitude. She looked Ezra dead in his eyes while taking his dick out of his boxers. Sunny held Ezra's dick in her hands and caressed it gently watching it grow and stiffen. "This is my fucking dick you understand me Ezra? Mine and no other bitch!" Sunny said while firmly yanking Ezra's dick. "Shit baby, you know it's yours. Daddy dick belongs to you baby."

Sunny was suddenly very turned on and her juices soaked her panties. She spit on the head of Ezra's dick and rammed his dick down her throat ignoring her gag reflexes. She began to vigorously bob up and down deep throating the shit out of Ezra's dick. " Waa waa Wait baby you gon make me cum too fast! Shit, wait! AAAAAAAAAAAAHHHHHHH FUCK!!!!" Ezra was so excited he pulled back fast causing his dick to slip out of Sunny's throat and his nut exploded onto Sunny's face. "Mmmmm....It taste so good E" as Sunny wiped his cum from her face; licking the sperm off her fingers. "That's right, swallow that shit. Every fucking drop" Ezra said out of breath. Ezra pulled his pants up while Sunny went into the bathroom in the basement to wash her face. As she closed the door and turned on the water she caught a glimpse of herself in the mirror, "What the fuck is wrong with me? How did I end up here?"

Sunny became sick to her stomach. She tried to dismiss the disturbing thoughts rushing into her mind. She felt used and abused. She didn't know who she was anymore. She felt completely lost. "I love him though. I really fucked up. It's my fault. I pushed him over the edge. I need a blunt."

6

In the coming weeks Sunny fell completely behind in school. It was hard for her to concentrate on homework and exams. Ezra kept her on a short leash. He made her check in with him whenever she was out of his sight. She felt this was his way of showing her he loved her and she liked every bit of it. Class was over and Sunny slept thru the entire lecture. She's been extremely fatigued for the past week. "Fuck, I'm sleepy as hell. I nced to start taking my ass home instead of fucking Ezra all night every night, shit" Sunny mumbled quietly to herself as she gathered her books and head to the door.

"Excuse me. Sweetheart, excuse me!" A classmate of Sunny's yelled out to her. He was a tall, milk chocolate, handsome man. This tantalizing man had to be about 220 lbs, 6'2" tall, bald head trimmed goatee with a thick dick print. "What's up?" Sunny asked eyeing the man up and down. "You forgot your notebook. Here you go." The young man handed Sunny her notebook. "Thanks." Sunny took the notebook and headed towards the door.

"So you live on campus?" Asked the handsome classmate. "Nope" Sunny replied speeding up her step becoming slightly annoyed. "So you must live in the area. My name is Ahmaad. Can I know yours? Or are you in a hurry?" "Sunny and yes I'm in a hurry." Sunny is totally irritated at this point. "I'm sorry I won't keep you. I just see you in class and I think you're one of the most attractive women on campus and I finally built up enough courage to introduce myself to you. I hope to see you in class next week, Sunny." Sunny was flattered and felt bad she was acting like a complete bitch. She pegged him as a male whore looking for the next piece of college ass with wack ass lines. "Thanks Ahmaad, I'll see you next week."

Sunny thought about Ahmaad all the way home. She didn't know why but she couldn't get him out of her head. He was such a gentleman and it didn't hurt that he was fine. BZZZ BZZZ BZZZ, Sunny's phone was vibrating in her purse. "Shit it's E. Ok this shit is starting to get old now." Sunny push the talk button, "Hey baby I'm on my way home what's up?" Sunny said dryly. "Sunny it's Shalisha. Don't hang up Sunny just hear me out please?" Sunny was shocked.

She didn't know what to think nor say. " Shalisha what the fuck do you want? It's been two months since you had my man's dick in your mouth and you got the balls to call me? Bitch, speak and make it quick!!" Sunny screamed into the receiver of her cell phone. "OK Sunny I deserve that and a lot more. I never got a chance to tell you how sorry I was. I know sorry don't mean shit to you but I miss you and our friendship. You are my sister and I know I fucked up I just had to call and tell you. I'm so sorry Sunny I miss you so fucking much.

That shit was not even worth it." Shalisha's voice was cracking as she struggled to get her words out. Sunny didn't know why but she felt bad for her friend. She could never hold grudges no matter how hard she tried. It just wasn't in her heart.

"Shalisha you right you did fuck up. I can't even be mad about the shit no more. I'll never trust you again, ever. I need to know some things" Sunny retorted. "I'll tell you whatever you want to know Sun." Shalisha obliged. "Did you fuck him, how many times and how did this shit start between yall two?" Sunny questioned Shalisha. "No we didn't fuck and that was our first sexual encounter. He started calling me one day out the blue talking about you and his problems and he begged me not to tell you. He knew what he was doing the whole time. He tried to bait me and my dumb ass took the bait because I was jealous of yall relationship. You know I ain't never had no steady man so I felt salty about the shit and I was on some hoe shit. He asked me to come over and blow one with him but I knew it was more to it and I came over and it happened. Sunny, I'm sorry. I'm so fucking sorry." Sunny was sitting in disbelief with tears streaming down her face. Shalisha I can't even fuck with you right now." **END CALL**.

All those feelings from that night resurfaced and she had to know why Ezra did that to her. It didn't make sense; she had to confront him. Sunny makes it home and she thanked God her parents are working late because she gets the house to herself. She

decides to take a shower before calling Ezra

over. Sunny steps out the shower and grabs her

towel. She sees a shadow outside the bathroom

window. Sunny is petrified and afraid to move.

"Open the damn door girl!" Ezra screams into

the bathroom window. "This muthafucka is

crazy!" Sunny thought to herself. "Hold on

shit!" Sunny grabs her robe and runs to the door

to let Ezra in, "Since when you start taking 30

minute showers?" Ezra questions Sunny with a

look of rage in his eyes. "What? Ezra what is

wrong with you? I just took a normal shower,

damn!" Ezra grabs Sunny by her arms and

swings her around as she tried to walk away

from him. "Bitch, you didn't go to school did

you? You think I'm stupid? You fucking

another nigga hoe?" Ezra says to sunny as spit

flies from his mouth into her face. "Nigga, let my arm go you tripping for real!!" WHAM! Ezra slaps Sunny. "Bitch I told you not to fuck with a nigga didn't I? Didn't I?" Sunny falls to the floor from the blow of Ezra's back hand to her face. She sits on the floor in disbelief; she can't believe he just back handed her. WHAM! "Aaaaahhhhh" Sunny screams in pain from Ezra's kick to her stomach. "Bitch get up! Where is the panties you just took off?! Get up and get them panties bitch!" Sunny is scared and in extreme pain. She tries to crawl to the bathroom to get the panties but she didn't move fast enough. Ezra grabs her by her hair and drags her into the bathroom. "Sunny, when I say move you move!" Ezra throws Sunny against the tub as they entered the bathroom.

He picks up her panties and inspects the crotch. He then smells the crotch of her panties and throws them on the ground. He walks to the toilet, sits down and puts his head in his hands. "What the fuck is wrong with me. What the fuck am I doing?" Ezra yells talking to himself. Sunny is in the fetal position moaning and crying in pain. She can't believe what Ezra just did to her. He never struck her before. He's choked her, but never beat her. She felt defeated and hopeless. She's never felt so low. "Baby, I'm sorry come here. Baby, come here. You alright baby? Get up" Ezra says to Sunny. "Get the fuck out Ezra. Get the fuck out!!" Sunny screams at Ezra. "Baby please I just thought when you didn't call me....baby I'm sorry. I'm sorry baby I won't trip like this again, baby come here." Ezra pleads. "Get the fuck out before I call the police nigga!! GET OUT!!!!" Ezra

steps over Sunny and leaves her parents' house.

Sunny lays on the bathroom floor and cries her

heart out. The side of her face is red and puffy.

"God please help me. I don't know what to do."

Sunny says a silent prayer to herself.

7

It has been four days since Ezra beat up Sunny. She has not returned any of his phone calls and she told her parents to tell him she's not home whenever he comes by. She's starting to miss him but she knows she should leave him for good. She gets in her car and heads down I-94 east to go to class and turns up the radio listening to Mason in the Morning. She was able to concentrate on the lecture given and take notes. She felt good and it's been a while since she felt good about school. She gathers her things as class is dismissed and sees Ahmaad.

"Hey, Ahmaad right?" Sunny asks knowing full well she remembered his name. "Yeah that's right." Ahmaad says showing all of his pearly white teeth. He seemed to be blushing, Sunny thought that was cute. "Sorry about last week. I probably was a bitch and I apologize." "No need for that, it's cool. We all have one of those days. I'm glad you spoke to me because if you didn't I probably would've never had the courage to say anything else to you." Ahmaad chuckles. "Oh really? You're a quitter huh? You shouldn't give up so easily. You'll be surprised how far persistence can get you" Sunny states boldly in an obviously flirtatious tone.

"Naw I'm not a quitter. I'm just not a bugaboo. So what do you have up today?" Ahmaad states as he continues to smile. "Oh, a little bit of this and that. You know how that goes." "Yeah well I'm on my way to work." Ahmaad says hoping Sunny ask him where he works so he can impress her. "Oh yeah? And just what do you do?" "I work for the 34th district. Just a file clerk nothing major but I got my foot in the door. I hope to be the head detective of homicide." Ahmaad proudly states. "That's what's up. Good for you, well I'll see you next week" Sunny states. "Before you go can I get your number?" Ahmaad boldly asks. "Hmm...No, I don't think so Ahmaad." Sunny states flatly. " OooKay may I ask why?" "I'm just not into quitters. See ya Ahmaad." Sunny gives him a wink and walks out of the auditorium.

Sunny walks to the parking lot and Ezra is standing next to her car. "Shit!" Sunny says under her breath as she walks towards him. "E, just leave me alone I'm not ready to see you." "Sunny I know I fucked up. I'm so sorry baby I just lost my temper. I haven't slept or ate shit in the past four days Sunny. I can't do shit until you forgive me and take me back. Baby I ain't shit without you. Sunny I might as well be dead if I don't have you in my life. You were made for me baby and I can't be without you. I'm gone get my shit straight just give me one more chance Sunny."

Ezra pleads to Sunny holding her arms while on bended knee. "E get up, you're drawing too much attention to yourself" Sunny says

while talking through her clinched teeth. "I
don't give a fuck I want all these muthafuckas to
know I ain't shit without you. Fuck them I need
you baby please put me out of my misery."
Sunny's heart softens and she feels special that
Ezra is willing to make a fool of himself to win
her back. She feels the love this man has for
her and it feels so damn good. It's like a drug
and she's addicted. "E, get up baby you know I
ain't going nowhere so just get up" Sunny says
smiling as on lookers shout awww. "Not until
you say you forgive me Sun." "Ezra, I forgive you
baby now get up!" Sunny says embarrassed.

Ezra gets up and gives Sunny a tender
kiss. "Oww Oww Oww" Shouts some onlookers.
Sunny was in heaven eating up all the attention
caused by her man. She caught a glimpsc of

Ahmaad as he winked at her and walked away.

"I'm gon follow you back to your house and I got a surprise for you." Ezra proudly tells Sunny. "What? What's the surprise?" Sunny ask anxiously. "You'll see, come on I'll trail you." Sunny is excited. She's singing and smiling all the way to her mom's house. She drops her car off and gets in the car with Ezra. She notices a bag in the back seat. "Ooh is my surprise in there?" As she quickly tries to grab the bag. "Get your hands off and wait Sun." Ezra says with a smirk on his face.

They pull up to Embassy Suite in Livonia. "Oooh baby you got us a room for the weekend?" Sunny says excitedly. "Yup I sure did. You been gone too long we got some making up to do." "Oh so you just knew I was gone take your monkey ass back huh? Nigga you make me sick" Sunny says with a light laugh. "Naw I didn't know fa sho but I was hoping and praying." The two get out of the car and Ezra grabs the bag out of the back seat and a suitcase from the trunk. Ezra checks in at the front desk and gets the key to their suite. "This is nice but it's nothing like the Pontchartrain. I'll never ever forget that night." Sunny says while planting a kiss on her man.

"Yeah this is tight though. Sit your fine ass down I want to show you what I got for you." Ezra pulls out a square shaped jewelry box. The box is too big for a ring. Sunny slowly opens it and it's a matching byzantine necklace and bracelet. Sunny screamed and jumped on Ezra kissing him all over his face. Sunny plants

kisses all over Ezra's face; Muah Muah Muah
"ooh baby I love it! This set you back a few
hundred, baby! How much crack you sell to buy
me this baby? ha ha ha!" "You know I work
hard for my girl. I had to stand on the block for
a while to get that for my baby. You like it
huh?" Ezra asked proudly. "Nigga, hell yeah
you know my taste. I'm bout to put it on now."
Sunny put on her new gift from her boyfriend
and admired it in the mirror. Ezra was proud of
himself. It made him feel good to do something
nice for his girlfriend. He always wanted his girl
to be laced and blinged out.

Ezra took the remainder of the contents in
the bag and laid them out on the bed. "Oh baby
you doing too much. You got me a teddy? So I
know I'm wearing that for you tonight huh?"

"Yeah you know it. I ain't had none of that good shit in over a week so you know I'm fiending" Ezra said as his dick began to grow in his pants. "I got some new shit for us to try babe, you down?" Ezra asked his girlfriend. "What new shit?"

8

"Ecstasy. I got two pills; one for you and one for me. It's the Pokémon kind so we should just take half this time." "I'ont know baby I'm scared." Sunny looked at the pills and contemplated on what to do. She took one out of the bag and said "fuck it, you only live once." Ezra broke the pill in half and place one half on Sunny's tongue and put the other half in his mouth. They sat on the bed to wait for the affects. "I don't feel any different." Sunny said unfazed. "It's only been five minutes Sun give it a minute" Ezra said amused by his impatient girlfriend. "Well I'm bout to take a shower ok?" Sunny kissed Ezra and headed for the shower.

Sunny likes her showers scalding hot so the bathroom was extremely foggy. She felt a heat wave travel through her body. It felt as if she was tingling from head to toe. She became extremely horny and aroused. She took her hand and started rubbing and pinching her nipples. She let out a moan. She thought to herself, "This shit finally kicked in." Ezra came into the bathroom, "Babe how you feeling?" "Horny as fuck! Get in here and get this pussy, E!" Sunny shouted over the shower door.

Ezra ripped his clothes off of him and jumped in the shower. His dick seemed to be two inches bigger and hard as steel. "E, please lick her. She missed you baby go ahead and give her a kiss." Ezra didn't utter a word. He got on his knees and put Sunny's left leg on his shoulder and devoured her pussy as if it was a five course meal. Sunny was even more turned on by the way he was moaning and groaning just from eating her pussy. She came so hard she went into convulsions. Ezra had to hold her waist to keep her from slipping. He stood up and tongued kissed Sunny like never before. They kissed so passionately they didn't notice the water turned ice cold. Ezra noticed Sunny shivering and cut the water off and wrapped her up in a towel. "You warming up, baby?" "I'm on fire E." Sunny said seductively biting her lower lip. Ezra sat the seat of the toilet down and sat on it, "Come and sit on daddy's dick."

Sunny obliged. She eased as much of Ezra's dick as she could into her tight wet pussy while letting out a moan. Sunny's pussy started to open up and adjust its fit around Ezra's dick; and as soon as she felt her pussy open for her man she started bouncing up and down on his dick. Her pussy juices were dripping down to his balls. Ezra held onto her waist tightly and made her stop in mid pump. He grabbed her legs, stood up and wrapped them around his waist. He stumbled towards the door and slammed Sunny's back into the door without hurting her. Sunny screamed from pleasure.

Ezra opened her ass cheeks to penetrate her pussy even deeper; and he started thrusting hard. You could hear his balls smacking against Sunny's ass. Sunny thought she was in heaven.

She was about to cum for the third time. "Oh shit baby....Aaahh daddy, I'm about to cum daddy. Oh shit Daddy, I'm cumming... I'm cumming oh shit ahhhhhhhhhhhhhhhhhhhh!" Sunny wrapped her arms around Ezra and sunk her teeth into his neck. It was as if she was possessed with a sex demon. Her creamy cum covered Ezra's dick, "I ain't no where near finished with you." Ezra panted. "Neither am I" Sunny said while sucking on her man's neck.

Ezra pulled his dick out, "Look at that good shit all on my dick baby. You see that shit?" Sunny said, "Yeah baby I see it; and that shit do look good. I want to taste it. Can I taste it baby?" Ezra liked the affects ecstasy had over Sunny. She was already a freak but now she was turning into a pornographic freak, and he loved it. "Hell yeah! Lick that shit baby." Sunny

got on her knees and slowly licked the bottom of

Ezra's dick all the way to the tip, "Mmmmm

fuck! My pussy taste so fucking good baby."

Ezra thought he would cum on himself right

then and there but the effects of ecstasy

wouldn't let him cum just yet. He felt like he

was going to explode.

Sunny continued to lick all sides of his

dick until it was clean. She then stood up,

grabbed his dick and lead him by his dick out of

the bathroom into the bedroom of the suite. "I

want you to fuck the shit out of me." Sunny

whispered in Ezra's ear. Ezra threw Sunny

down on the bed and told her to turn over on her

stomach. She did as he wished. Ezra grabbed

her hips in a manner that had her ass sticking

up in the air and she was on all fours. He took
his tongue and licked her ass crack as if it were
covered in honey. "Ooh fuck!!" Sunny shouted.
Ezra slapped Sunny's ass cheeks on both sides
so hard he left his hand imprint. He took his
hard dick in his hand and slowly stuck the head
into her wet throbbing pussy. He continued to
take it out and stick it back in. He enjoyed
watching his girl squirm from anticipation. He
took his dick out once more and waited a few
seconds and slowly but firmly slid all 8.5" of his
dick into Sunny's pussy.

She tried to fall flat but Ezra had her by
the waist. "Don't you run from this dick" Ezra
teased. Sunny moaned and squealed from the
pain and pleasure. Ezra got his stride going and
sweat started to drip down his chest. He was

putting in some serious work. He pulled his
dick out and turned Sunny over onto her back.
He lifted her legs and put them behind her head
as if she were a pretzel. He held on to the back
of her legs and guided his dick back inside her
soaking wet pussy. He loved watching his dick
go in and out, out and in.

His dick is covered from base to head with
creamy pussy juice. "Look at my dick going in
my pussy. Look at it" Ezra ordered Sunny.
"Baby I see that shit. Got damn E!!" Sunny was
about to cum again. She took her hand and
touched Ezra's dick as it was pumping in and
out of her pussy to see just how wet she was.
She thought she was going to pass out from
pleasure. She took her wet fingers and placed
them inside of Ezra's mouth and he sucked the

juices off her fingers until it was clean. "Sunny, I'm bout to cum. Oh shit, where you want this nut?" Ezra yelled. "I want it on my titties baby! Give it to me on my titties!" Sunny screamed back. Ezra quickly pulled his dick out with a drop of his cum seeping out as he pulled out. He barely made it to her breast.

"Grrrrrrrrrrrrrrrrrrrrrrrr AAHHHHHHHHHHHHHH FUCK!"

Ezra nutted all over Sunny's tits. She rubbed it in enjoying every minute. Ezra collapsed next to her breathing heavily. "I missed your muthafucking ass. Don't ever leave me for that long" Ezra told Sunny. "I promise baby I won't." The two lay in bed for the next hour trying to re-cooperate. Sunny's phone rang and Ezra sat up and looked at Sunny as if she were psychic and knew who was calling her.

She hunched her shoulders as to suggest she

didn't know. Ezra got up and looked at the

screen on her cell phone.

"What the fuck is Shalisha calling you

for?" Ezra asked Sunny. "She called the night

we got into it and apologized for fucking you."

"We didn't fuck Sun" Ezra said irritated. "You

might as well" Sunny said with an attitude. "I

should tell her to come up here so I can see you

fuck her." Sunny said with a slight tone of

disdain in her voice. "Shut the fuck up Sunny.

We having a good time don't ruin it" Ezra

retorted back. "Baby I'm serious I want to see

you fuck her. I want her to lick my pussy too. I

want to see what you like about her and why

you were willing to risk losing mc." "I wasn't

gone fuck that girl I just wanted my dick sucked. And she ain't got shit on you; she just another rat baby. You know a nigga gone do what he gone do." "Still, I want you to fuck her" Sunny demanded. "Man that X got you tripping. You on some ill shit."

Sunny was hell bent on getting Ezra to fold. She wanted to see Ezra have sex with a woman he was obviously willing to lose it all for. She didn't know why she felt this way and where it was coming from but it was something inside of her that couldn't let it go. "I'm calling her back E. I want to do this for you. I mean I don't want no secrets between us and I definitely don't want you fucking around on me behind my back." Ezra looked at his girlfriend with pure confusion. "Sun I'm not feeling that shit. I just want you and you only. I can't share you; I don't want no other bitch but you." Ezra replied back to Sunny. "Oh, so now you calling me a bitch?" Sunny stated sarcastically. "Sun quit tripping you know what I'm saying, shit. You bout to blow my high with this shit." Sunny laughed. She knew she was getting to Ezra.

She and Ezra lay down on the bed and smoked an L. Ezra drifted off to sleep but Sunny was wide awake and high as a kite. She can't stop thinking about Shalisha and why she was calling. She grabbed her cell phone and went through the missed call list and hit dial. "What's up Lisha, what do you want?" Sunny says dryly through the receiver, "Sunny I'm glad you called me back. I just wanted to know if we were cool? I really miss you." Shalisha says pathetically.

"Yeah I'm straight on that. It's over and done with Lisha." "Sunny oh my God, are you serious? I thought you was gon hate my ass forever. I'm about to cry."

Sunny really did miss her friend but she had other things in mind at this point and time. "So where you at Lisha? What you doing?" "I'm at home, I don't have nothing going on tonight. Where you at? You want to go out tonight?" Shalisha asked eagerly. "No, me and E is up here at the Embassy Suites in Livonia. You want to come through?" Sunny asked boldly. "Um Sunny, why do I want to come to a room with you and your man? That ain't even right Sunny. You trying to pull one over on me?" Shalisha states with a fearful tone in her voice. "Bitch stop tripping. Look I'm gon keep it real with you. I'm high as fuck Lish. Me and E took some ecstasy tonight and when you called I told him I wanted you to come up here and fuck us. Don't trip cause I'm not. I just want you to fuck me and I want to see him fuck you. I'm not holding any punches this is what I want so, what do you think?"

Shalisha was completely silent. She was trying to wrap her mind around this entire situation and she didn't understand why Sunny did a complete 180 degree turn. "But, Sunny I don't want to fuck Ezra. When I called you to apologize I meant that shit. Our friendship is worth so much more." Sunny had tunnel vision, at this point she wanted what she wanted and she's willing to do whatever to get what she wants. Not taking into account the consequences of opening pandora's box.

"Shalisha, I appreciate what you're saying and I forgive you for everything but I'm on some different shit right now. I'm a freak Lisha, you know this and I just think we would have a good time with each other. No one has to know. You only live once so, why not? And who else will offer you a situation like this? You've known both of us forever. You're attracted to at least one of us so, why not? You owe me anyway!" Sunny said over the phone almost whispering so Ezra didn't hear what she was up to. Shalisha paused for what seem to be hours. "Hello!" Sunny yelled into the receiver. "I'm here, damn! Ok, fuck it. What's your room number?" Shalisha answered. "222 and hurry up Lisha with your slow ass!" Sunny ended the call.

Sunny is filled with excitement and lust. Sunny gets what Sunny wants.

She crept out of the bathroom as to not disturb Ezra and sure enough he's snoring his ass off still. Sunny gently gets back into bed with him and starts to softly trace his chest and abs with her fingertips. She wasn't getting the response she wanted so she started to massage his dick. She watches as Ezra dicks grows and stiffens and she's completely turned on. But, she doesn't want to have sex with him yet. She wants to get him so completely horny and turned on that he would fuck anything just to get his nut out.

Ezra wakes up, "Baby you ready for some more daddy dick?" Ezra seductively asks sunny. "Not yet daddy I just want to massage you and make you feel nice and relaxed" Sunny responded to Ezra almost in a whisper. Sunny continues to massage Ezra's dick and she moves on to other parts of his body making Ezra's toes curls. It was as if Sunny was sending shock waves through his entire body. *Knock Knock Knock* Who the fuck is that? I hope it ain't security because we're smoking? "Ezra said seeming concerned. "Baby calm down, I know who it is. Hold up while I get the door; just lay down." Sunny puts on Ezra's t-shirt and opens the door.

9

"Hey honey" Sunny said to Shalisha. "I'm glad you came!" "I almost didn't but anything for you Sun" Shalisha said speaking in a nervous tone. Ezra sat straight up in the bed. His eyes were as big as half dollars but he didn't utter a word. Shalisha couldn't even look at Ezra, she felt ashamed still. "Why is everybody so quiet? We need to loosen up a bit and fix us all a drink. I'm thirsty as hell off this shit anyway" Sunny said. "Yeah baby you got to drink a lot of juice when you gone off E. Fix me a double baby" Ezra told Sunny. "Me too"

Shalisha said. Sunny fixed everybody a drink

and turned on the clock radio for some music.

After a few drinks everyone loosened up and

they were all laughing and joking having a good

time. "Shalisha, do you want to try this

pokemon pill?" Sunny asked her friend. "I don't

know Sun, I'm not really into that shit. I'm a

little noided." Ezra chimed in, "It ain't shit to be

noided about. This shit will have you feeling

right. You and Sun can take the last one."

Shalisha was scared; but, she trusted Sunny.

She felt in her heart Sunny wouldn't let anything

happen to her that she didn't want. "Fuck it,

give me the pill."

Sunny got the ecstasy pill, broke it in half

and placed one half on Shalisha' s tongue and

the other half in her mouth. They continued to drink and laugh about everything under the sun until Soulful Moaning by Dale came on the clock radio. Shalisha moaned, "Ooh this is my shit!" Shalisha got up and started doing a seductive dance to soulful moaning. She started to roll her hips and pop her ass better than any stripper Ezra and Sunny's ever seen. Sunny walked over to Ezra and sat on his lap. She whispered in his ear, "We're gonna have a good time fucking her baby." Ezra grabbed Sunny's face and started kissing her passionately. Sunny pulled away and started to dance with Shalisha seductively. Sunny pulled Shalisha by her waist and kissed her lips gently. Shalisha's body responded. Her breathing became heavy. Sunny slowly took Shalisha's shirt off along with her jeans.

Shalisha's standing there with nothing but her bra and panties on. Ezra's sitting on the bed enjoying the show. "Sunny, I want to taste you." Shalisha said. Sunny smiled and said, "You will baby. Take off your panties and bra but do it slowly." Sunny was clearly in charge. Shalisha did exactly what Sunny told her to do. Sunny motioned for Shalisha to lie on the bed next to Ezra. "Lisha, I want you to suck his dick." Shalisha didn't say a word she did whatever Sunny commanded her to do. Shalisha starts to suck Ezra's hard dick and Sunny straddles his face.

There's nothing but moans and sucking noises in the air. Sunny's pussy explodes with cum all over Ezra's face; and he has a tight grip on her hips to ensure she doesn't move.

Shalisha stops sucking his dick and pries his hands off Sunnys hips. She pushes Sunny down on the bed and starts sucking her nipples. Shalisha's never been with a woman, but you can't tell because she knows what she's doing. She licks Sunny from head to toe leaving her pussy the last part on her body to devour. Ezra gets out of the bed and sits in a chair to watch the show. Shalisha gently pushes Sunny's legs open and slowly plant kisses along her inner thighs. She finally gets to Sunny's creamy center and she begins to fuck Sunny with her tongue. Sunny is moaning and her legs begin to shake. "Shalisha what the fuck are you doing to me? Oh God this feels so fucking good! Fuck!" Sunny screams.

Ezra feels left out. He's turned on but he's

been sitting long enough. He gets up and walks over to the bed. He pulls Shalisha by her hair and forces his tongue down her throat. "I want you to get the fuck off my girl and lick my ass." Ezra lets Shalisha's hair go and dives into Sunny's pussy. Shalisha gets behind Ezra and starts doing exactly what he told her to do. It's hard for him to concentrate on Sunny because he's about to blow. Just before he climaxes Sunny gets up and pushes Shalisha off of him.

"You're a nasty bitch! Get the fuck out!" Sunny screams. "What the fuck Sunny? What the fuck are you doing?" Ezra shouts. Shalisha is standing there in a state of shock. She's confused and doesn't know if she should run out of the room naked or start putting her clothes on. "E you shut the fuck up! Bitch I said get the fuck out before I beat your ass! I'm not playing

Shalisha!" Shalisha doesn't utter a word. She

throws her clothes on and heads out the door

but not before slamming it. "I can't believe this

shit. What the fuck am I doing? What the fuck

did I just do?" Sunny starts talking to herself.

"I told you I didn't want to do this. And now

that I'm doing what you wanted you're gonna

bug the fuck out? What the fuck did you think

was gon happen Sunny? Huh? This shit is your

fucking fault. You can't handle this shit you

shouldn't have started it." Ezra scolds Sunny.

"E I'm not trying to hear that shit just take

me home. I'm ready to go home now." Sunny

you must be out your fucking mind. I ain't

taking your ass nowhere. Your ass can walk

home! You brought this shit on yourself."

Sunny doesn't say another word. She starts getting her things together because she can't take the sight of Ezra. "You really think I'm gon' let you walk home? Sunny?! You ain't leaving nowhere just lay your ass down and go to sleep. You seriously tripping! You know what's fucked up? You did this shit with Tyra and some random ass nigga but you can't even get down with your man? I should fuck you up just off that alone."

Something inside of Sunny snapped. She got tired of the threats and the abuse she has taken from Ezra and herself. She ties her last shoe string on her air ones and gets up and looks Ezra dead in the eyes and clocks him in the mouth. She begins to kick and punch and stomp Ezra in his nuts, "I fucking hate you!

Look at what you did to me! I'm this way
because of your bitch ass! Fuck you nigga! Fuck
you!" She caught Ezra completely off guard and
he's stunned and shocked rolling around on the
floor. "Bitch I'm going to kill you *cough*
cough" Sunny knows she has a short amount
of time before Ezra gets up from the floor. She
grabs all of her things and darts out of the door.
She calls Tyra and tells her to come and get her
from the gas station up the street. Tyra is there
within 15 minutes.

As soon as Sunny gets in the car she
starts crying her eyes out while telling Tyra the
entire story. "Sunny, you need to leave Ezra
alone. You two are going to kill each other. This
relationship is so toxic and fucked up, you're
losing yourself. I don't even know who you are

anymore Sunny! And God forbid if you have a baby by this nigga! Get out while you still have a chance Sunny and focus on you and get your shit together!" Tyra is extremely concerned for her best friend. This is the lowest she's ever seen her. "You're right T. I'm too young and I have the whole world ahead of me to be caught up by some street nigga." The rest of the ride home was quiet. Sunny just stared out the window trying to pull herself together. She knew the next time she saw Ezra it wouldn't be pretty. "Well you're home girl. You're more than welcomed to come to my house if you want to you know that, right Sunny?" "Yeah T I know. Thank you for everything ok?" Sunny leans over and gives Tyra a kiss goodbye.

Sunny hoped she wouldn't wake her

mother. It's 3am and the last thing she needed was an argument with her mom. "Sunny we need to talk!" Her mother shouted from her bedroom. "Shit!" Sunny whispered to herself. "Now look, I know you're 18 and you *THINK* you're grown but this is my house. You will not come tip toeing in here whenever you like. I got to get up in the morning and go to work. I don't need to be disturbed by you sneaking in all hours of the night doing God knows what with those raggedy niggas you run around with! Either you come in by 1am or you need to get your own shit. Live on campus or something but you need to figure this shit out!" Sunny was too tired and defeated to put up a fight and besides she knew her mother was right deep down but of course she wouldn't admit it. "Alright Ma, I'll move out." Sunny said in a dry tone. Sunny's mother looked shocked. "How in the hell are you going to move any damn where! You don't have a job and you're going to school! You just need to follow the rules Sunny!" Sunny didn't want to argue. "Okay Ma. I hear you. I'll do better. Goodnight." Sunny kissed her mother on the cheek, went in her room and lay across her bed and passed out.

10

It's been almost two weeks and Sunny

hasn't spoken to Ezra or Shalisha. Rumor has it

Ezra and Shalisha are dating. They were

spotted at a Coney Island restaurant one late

night. Sunny seemed unaffected. Almost

relieved because maybe this was the out she was

praying for. Final exams were fast approaching

and Sunny has a lot on her plate. She

desperately wants to move out of her parents'

home, she needs a job and she has to pull a b

average on her exams. She decides to go to the campus library to study hard core for her pre-calculus exam. Sunny hates math and wishes she had a tutor.

"Mind if I share your table?" A deep whisper filled Sunny's ear and the smell of Issey Miyake filled her nose. Sunny looked up and saw the whisper came from Ahmaad. "Not at all. Maybe you can help me with our pre-cal exam." Sunny whispered back. "It would be my pleasure. " Sunny and Ahmaad studied for about 4 hours straight. They both were exhausted. "Hey, you wanna grab a bite to eat? I could go for a corned beef sandwich" Ahmaad asked Sunny. "That sounds so good I'm starving. "

They gathered their books and headed to

the parking lot. "You wanna ride with me? I'll

bring you back to your car. It doesn't make

sense for both of us to drive." Ahmaad asked

Sunny. "Ok." Ahmaad was a complete

gentleman. He opened the car door for Sunny

and she was impressed. "You have good

manners; good job, Ahmaad" Sunny said in a

joking manner. "My father taught me well. So I

haven't seen you in class much; is everything

good with you Sunny?" "Yeah... Well everything

is good now. Just dealing with a lot of stuff

back home. I'm looking for an apartment and I

desperately need a job. Life is just a struggle

right now, you know?" Ahmaad stopped at the

red light and looked Sunny in her eyes. "I'm

proud of you. Despite what you're going through

you still manage to study and make time for

school. It'll get better just keep your head up.

You're a smart woman Sunny. You're different. I mean that in the most respectful way possible." Sunny giggled. "I appreciate that Ahmaad. Thank you. And you're pretty different yourself; In a good way."

Ahmaad and Sunny ate and talked at the restaurant for hours. They laughed and talked about their upbringing, goals and past relationships. Sunny was really enjoying his company. She's never gone out with a guy quite like Ahmaad. He never tried anything with her; which turned her on even more. He intrigued her and the feelings were mutual. "I think we should leave before they kick us out. Do you have to go home?" Asked Ahmaad. "No not yet. I'm enjoying my time with you Ahmaad. I really am. Did you have something in mind?"

Ahmaad was excited she still wanted to chill with him. "I just thought it would be a good idea to walk this sandwich off ha! You want to go to Belle Isle and look at the water?" Sunny started feeling butterflies in her stomach, "I would like that Ahmaad." Sunny and Ahmaad walked around the island and just took in the beauty of the city lights. "Man this is such a nice night. Thank you Ahmaad." Ahmaad turned to Sunny, "Sunny there's nothing to thank me for; I should be thanking you. You're like a breath of fresh air. I hope we can do this again sometime soon." Sunny bit her bottom lip in a flirtatious manner. "So do I Ahmaad. I think I should head back to my car it's getting late."

On the ride back to the parking lot to retrieve Sunny's car, Ahmaad and Sunny held hands the entire time. He asked about Ezra and Sunny told him they were history. She didn't go into great detail but that's all Ahmaad wanted to know. Ahmaad parked next to Sunny's car and he gets out opening her door. "Thanks again Ahmaad. You don't know how much I needed this." Before Ahmaad could respond Sunny leans in gently, grabs his chin, pulls him to her lips and plants a gentle yet passionate kiss. "Aaaannytime Sunny." Ahmaad stutters. "Dag girl you got me stuttering!" They both broke out in a laugh.

They exchanged numbers and go their separate ways. Sunny is glowing on the ride home. Sunny decides to get some gas before she goes home so she won't have to do it in the morning. She finishes pumping her gas and she sees Ezra and Shalisha pulling up in Shalisha's car. Sunny goes cold. She just stands there and looks. Shalisha has a smirk on her face and Ezra has a blank stare. Sunny doesn't utter a word she gets in her car and goes home. Not more than five minutes later Ezra starts calling her nonstop. Sunny refuses to answer. She is finally done with Ezra and all of his bullshit. She deserves better. Ahmaad just might be the better man.

Four weeks has passed since Ahmaad and Sunny's first date and they've been seeing each other every day going forward. Sunny hasn't slept with Ahmaad yet but she thinks it's time. She's ready to see what he's working with. Ahmaad is coming out to pick her up from her parents' house for their one month anniversary.

They're both corny like that. Ahmaad rings the door bell and her mother answers. Sunny doesn't rush out yet she wants to listen to their conversation. He's extremely polite to her mother. Yes ma'am no ma'am.

Sunny is tickled pink. She decides her mother has tortured him enough so she makes her grand entrance. "Hey Ahmaad." Ahmaad looks at Sunny and he's stunned by how beautiful she looks. Sunny is wearing a fitted black halter dress that shows off all of her curves. Her hair is pinned up with a few loose curls flowing down her shoulders. Her skin is flawless. The only makeup she has on is eye shadow and lip gloss. She's stunning. "You look beautiful Sunny. Are we ready?" Ahmaad says. "Yep, I'm all set. See you later Ma."

Sunny's mother likes Ahmaad. Her faith is beginning to be restored in her daughters taste in men. "Alright, yall have fun and be careful!" Sunny mother states matter of factly.

Sunny and Ahmaad dined at Fishbones restaurant in Downtown Detroit. The food was excellent. After dinner Ahmaad felt like dancing the night away. "Baby, do you want to try this new club? It's called Bosco. You have to be 21 to get in but I know the doorman I can definitely get you in." Sunny was all smiles. "I'm down. Let's go!" The couple arrived at the club and got in with ease: as the doorman gave Ahmaad dap, admiring his lovely lady. The setup of the club was sophisticated and chill. Couches against the wall, red lights are on; it's very grown and sexy. Ahmaad ordered two dirty martinis. Sunny never drank a dirty martini. She's accustomed to Seagrams and Hennessy. She's never been able to order a drink at the bar because she's not 21 yet. She's definitely feeling herself right now. "Baby this taste so good! I like this spot too. Very sexy!" Ahmaad just smiled, "I'm glad you like it baby. Let's dance." They both danced until their feet hurt and the club was closing. "Baby my feet are killing me! Let's go back to your place. Is your roommate home?" Ahmaad wanted to race home but he tried to keep his cool. "Naw juice is gone for the weekend bae. It's just me and you."

The two get back to Ahmaads apartment. Sunny sits on the couch and takes her heels off. "Another perfect night with Mr. Ahmaad Jackson. Come here baby." Ahmaad walks over

to Sunny and gets on his knees. He grabs her
foot and starts to give her a foot massage.
Sunny puts her head back and enjoys every
second of being pampered. She stands up and
asks, "Baby can you unzip my dress for me?"
Ahmaad does exactly what she says. Sunny is
standing in his living room with nothing on but
her bra and panties.

Ahmaad steps back and just looks at
Sunny. "You're so fucking beautiful Sunny. I
want you so bad right now." Sunny looks at
Ahmaad seductively and says, "You can have me
Ahmaad. I'm all yours tonight." Ahmaad grabs
Sunny's hand and leads her to his bedroom.
She undresses him slowly. His 9 inch dick is
rock hard. She then takes her bra off and
throws it on the floor. Ahmaad starts to kiss

and suck on her breast as he slowly slides her panties down. "I want to make love to you Sunny. " Ahmaad motions for Sunny to lie down on his bed. He gets on top of her and kisses her passionately. He traces his tongue all over her body. "Ahmaad I can't take it baby I need to feel you inside of me." Sunny begs. "You will baby. I want to take my time with you." Ahmaad begins to suck on her toes. Surprisingly Sunny is turned on by this. She then takes her toes out of his mouth and motions for him to lie down. She gives him the most incredible massage.

Ahmaad is so turned on, pre cum starts to drip from the tip of his dick. Ahmaad grabs Sunny and gets on top of her. "Sunny look at me; I love you. I'm in love with you. Don't say anything, I just want you to know how I truly feel." Sunny smiles from ear to ear and she kisses him tenderly. Ahmaad reaches for a condom out of his drawer and Sunny takes it from him. "I got this." Sunny said. She opens the condom and puts it in her mouth. Ahmaad is watching in amazement. Sunny puts the condom on his dick with her mouth. Ahmaad wants to explode but he's trying to hold it together. Sunny gets on top and slowly guides his dick inside of her soaking wet pussy.

They both let out moans. Sunny starts to rock back and forth on his dick: trying to accommodate the size of his dick inside of her pussy. She picks up momentum and she leans over and starts kissing him while her ass is bouncing up and down on his dick. Ahmaad grabs her ass cheeks to make his dick go as deep as it can go inside her pussy. "Oooh shit! Ahmaad, oh fuck baby!" Sunny screams in pain and pleasure. Ahmaad then grabs Sunny's waist and gets her to lie on her side. He lifts her leg towards his head board and starts thrusting against her pussy. You can hear his balls slapping against her soaking wet pussy.

"Oh fuck Ahmaad...Ahmaad I'm about to cum baby! Ahmaad, I'm cuming! Ahhhh fuck!!" Sunny cums all over Ahmaads nine inch dick. Sunny is shaking uncontrollably, biting his pillow. Ahmaad snatches the pillow away from her and kisses her passionately. He then gets on top of her and slowly pulls his dick out then in: Picking up speed and force with each thrust. "Fuck Sunny! Got damnit baby I'm about to nut, fuck!" Ahmaad explodes from climaxing. His sperm filled the condom. He slowly pulls his dick out with quiet whimpers because his dick is extremely sensitive after an orgasm like this. He lies next to Sunny and puts her head on his chest and they both fell fast asleep.

It's about 5am in the morning and Sunny awakes. Ahmaad is sound asleep. She runs to the bathroom and starts to vomit. Ahmaad comes in the bathroom, "Bae are you ok?" Sunny manages to talk, "I think it was the seafood baby! I don't feel well." Ahmaad gets her a glass of water and a wash cloth to wash her face. "I'm going to get you home baby you think you can make it in the car?" Ahmaad asked concerned. "Yeah, I'll be fine." Ahmaad drives

Sunny home as she slept the entire way. "Baby we're here. Call me if you need anything ok?" Ahmaad says. "Ok baby I will I just need to rest I think." Sunny kisses her new man and goes into her parents' house and passes out on the bed.

11

Sunny has been sick for the past two days and decides to go to the doctors for food poisoning. "Well Sunny it looks like you're pregnant!" Says Dr. Armstrong. "What? Excuse me? What did you say?" Dr. Armstrong grabs Sunny's shoulder and say, "you're pregnant Sunny. You haven't had your period in two months so you seem to be right around 10 weeks. You definitely still have options. Do you know what you want to do?" Sunny starts bawling her eyes out. "No! No I can't be! I'm in school! I just started dating a great man! I live with my parents! I can't have a baby!"

Dr. Armstrong heart goes out to Sunny. "Sunny, women have options. If this is something you don't want to go through we can take steps to terminate the pregnancy, but we don't have a lot of time. Think about it ok? Take this pamphlet. It talks about all of your options." Sunny is still crying and in a state of shock. "Ok Doc. OK." The doctor leaves out and Sunny sits on the doctors table staring at the walls in disbelief. She finally gets dressed and goes home.

Ahmaad has been calling her for the past week but she can't seem to face him. She doesn't know what to say or if she should say anything. She calls Tyra and tells her everything and ask for advice. "Sun a baby is a blessing. I don't know how you would handle killing your first born baby. I'm here for you with whatever you decide but you got to own up to your responsibilities." Sunny was quiet and she realized Tyra made some valid points. She found herself rubbing her stomach. "You're right T. I got some praying to do. I'll talk to you later T. Bye." Sunny hangs up the phone. Sunny wants to tell Ezra so bad but she doesn't know how. "Fuck it I'm just going to tell him." Ezra picks up the phone. "Hello." Sunny voice is shaky. "E I'm pregnant."

"Say what? What the fuck you telling me this bullshit for, Sunny?" Sunny can feel her anger rise, but she knows she must keep her composure. She can't allow Ezra to control this conversation. "E, I'm telling you because it's your baby. I'm' ten weeks pregnant. You don't have to say or do anything. I thought you should know. Goodbye." Sunny hangs up the phone feeling even more confused. She stares at her phone assuming Ezra would start blowing up her phone. But, it doesn't ring. Two hours has passed and he hasn't called nor text sunny.

DING DONG

Sunny is startled by the doorbell as the sound breaks her from her trance. She looks out of the peep hole and low and behold it's...Ezra. Sunny instantly gets butterflies and feels anxious, excited, nervous, scared and angry all at once. All of these emotions start to drown her. She starts breathing heavily.

DING DONG DING DONG

Sunny runs to the bathroom and splashes water on her face. She looks at herself in the mirror. "Sunny pull yourself together. Pull it together!" She opens the door and Ezra is walking back towards his car. Sunny opens the door and Ezra turns around as he hears the door open. He stood still and stared for what seemed an eternity. Sunny motions for him to come inside. Ezra comes inside and goes downstairs without being told to do so and takes a seat on the couch. Sunny follows. She feels nervous. Her palms began to sweat. She doesn't know what to expect.

"Sunny, you can't kill my baby. I want my baby. I need my family. I need you Sunny. If this isn't a sign from God that we should be together then I don't know what is, Sunny.

Fuck everything we've done and who we've done it with. The game has changed. You are having my baby; my first born. Let's make shit right sunny." Sunny listens silently while tears pour down her cheeks. Ezra scoots closer to Sunny on the couch and wraps his arms around her as he wipes the tears from her face. He kisses her forehead and they both start to cry.

"Ezra what are we going to do with a baby? I just finished my first year of college. I don't have a job, and you're a fucking drug dealer. I live with my mom and you with your granny. How can we possibly make it E? How? Not to mention all the fucked up shit that's happened between us. This is a recipe for calamity. Ezra I'm so fucking scared. I'm scared E!!!" Ezra grabs Sunny's face. "Snap out of this shit Sunny and boss up. You ain't ever been

afraid of shit. You've overcome some fucked up

shit in your life and you're telling me you're

scared of a baby? Our baby? Our perfect baby,

that God has blessed us with? Get over yourself

for real. This is fate. We are meant to be. I will

do everything in my power to get us up out this

bitch and have a good life. Give my baby a

chance. "

Sunny feels a sense of relief and calm and

for the first time she feels certain of what she

wants to do. She's going to be a mommy. The

love she had for Ezra resurfaces. It never went

away she was just masking it with Ahmaad...

Ahmaad. Sunny instantly felt sick to her

stomach. She got so wrapped up into this

moment with Ezra she completely forgot about

everything she and Ahmaad had on the table.
She'd never met a man like Ahmaad. Their
future seemed a lot more promising and bright
compared to the life she would have with Ezra.
But, did she really know Ahmaad? After all it's
only been a month.

She couldn't help but wonder how their
story would unfold. "I'm pregnant with E's baby.
What am I thinking?" Sunny thinks to herself.
She's feeling overwhelmed. "E, we have a lot to
talk about and figure out but, I want to get some
rest for today. I'll come by tomorrow ok?" Ezra
just stares at Sunny. He looks as if his feelings
are hurt. As if he's disappointed. "I ain't seen
you in over a month Sun. Damn I miss you. I
thought we could talk some more but alright I'll
let you get your rest." Sunny feels relieved but a

bit of guilt. "Hey, I've missed you too. Tomorrow, and every day after; I promise." Sunny grabs Ezra's chin, nibbles on his bottom lip and kisses him seductively. She knew exactly how to make Ezra melt like butter. He was putty in her hands. Ezra kisses her back and leaves her parents' house.

"What am I going to say to Ahmaad? I have to see him. I have to tell him in person. He deserves this much." Sunny text Ahmaad and ask if she can come by to talk to him. He responds immediately. He replies with a simple, "yeah." He's obviously annoyed and confused by Sunny ignoring him for the past week after their amazing night. Sunny gets in the shower and rehearses what she's going to say to Ahmaad over and over. It's a beautiful summer's night and Sunny is thankful for the 30 minute drive to the riverfront apartment's Downtown Detroit. Gives her time to really think about what she wants to say and how she should say it.

Buzzzzzzz

"Who is it?" Yells Ahmaad thru the intercom. "It's Sunny, Ahmaad."

Buzzzzzzzzzzzzzzzzzzzzzzzzzzzzzzzzzzzzzz

Ahmaad buzzes Sunny up and he's pacing the floor anticipating this conversation. He's thinking maybe he scared her off because he confessed his love for her. Too soon, too fast. So many thoughts raced thru his mind. She walked thru the door; she was glowing and smelled like candy land. He was so smitten by her beauty. He forgot about how angry he had been; how confused she made him, and how embarrassed he had been.

He walked up to her, grabbed her face tongued her down right there in the door way. He couldn't control himself, and Sunny didn't stop him. He tore Sunny's dress from her body: Causing the buttons from the front of the sundress to fly all over the floor. She didn't have on any panties and he dove right in to her sweet creamy center. Sunny was in disbelief. She couldn't stop him because she needed to feel this type of connection. She needed this release; desperately. She let Ahmaad have his way with her.

After they both climaxed, Ahmaad and Sunny lay in his bed breathless staring at the ceiling. Sunny is thinking she can't possibly tell

Ahmaad after this. She didn't know what to do.
"So talk to me Sun. Why the cold shoulder for
the past week? Did I run you off?" Sunny didn't
want to lie to Ahmaad. She didn't have it in her
to betray him because he's been nothing but
good to her. She felt the need to put on her
proverbial big girl drawls and boss up.

"Ahmaad I'm pregnant. 10 weeks and it's
Ezra's, my ex. I found out after I got sick over
here. I'm sorry Ahmaad." Sunny blurted this
life altering news out and she just continued to
stare at the ceiling. She couldn't stomach
looking Ahmaad in his eyes. She felt ashamed,
embarrassed and overwhelmingly sad because,
she genuinely had great affection for Ahmaad.
She wasn't in love with him but she knew
Ahmaad had what it took to sweep her off her

feet and win her heart.

Ahmaad sat up in his bed in silence and just stared at Sunny. Tears started to flow down Sunny's face. Ahmaad felt like he'd been hit by a freight train. He was in utter disbelief. He didn't know if he should be angry, sad, relieved the baby wasn't his, hurt, offer to help. He just didn't know. "Sunny I don't know what to say. I feel like I've been hit with a ton of bricks. Just the other night...our night, our perfect night: I told you I love you for the first time and had the best sex I've ever had in my life. And now you're telling me you're pregnant with your ex's baby? I'm assuming you're keeping the baby because why else would you tell me. Right?" Sunny wiped the tears from her eyes got out of the bed and put her ripped sundress on. "Right. I'm

sorry for everything. I wish things were different.
I'm sorry I hurt you Ahmaad."

Sunny felt angry for some reason. So
many emotions raced through both of them.
Ahmaad didn't want Sunny to leave. He didn't
want to lose her despite her carrying another
man's baby. That was the only thing he knew
for certain. "Sunny stop: just fucking stop.
Don't run out on me. You left me hanging in the
wind for the past week and now you drop this
bomb on me and you're running out of my life? I
don't deserve to talk to you? To figure this out
together?

I'm in love with you woman. I don't say
shit I don't mean. When I love, I love hard. You
turned my world upside down Sunny. I don't
want to lose you. I don't know what that means

for you, but I know I don't want you out of my life. Talk to me Sunny. After all the shit this nigga put you through, you thinking about giving him another chance because of a baby? What do you think this baby is going to do? Change him? Sunny talk to me got damnit! Say something!" Sunny stood in the middle of Ahmaads bedroom with her ripped sundress blowing in the wind from the ceiling fan. Her swollen breast and hard nipples standing at attention: looking Ahmaad in his eyes. Her pussy damped with sweat and cum. Glistening from the street lights out of the window. Her arms down her side and her face stoic.

"Ahmaad, you don't know what you're saying. You don't know how you'll feel a month from now. Nine months from now. How will you explain to your family? The woman you love is pregnant with another man's baby. How does that look? And maybe MY baby will change Ezra. You aren't a fortune teller. Just because I've told you some fucked up shit that transpired between us doesn't give you the right to judge his character or what he's capable of doing."

Ahmaad snapped, "Are you really defending this nigga to me? After everything, you're defending him? So you still love him obviously. Were you just using me to get over this bum ass nigga, Sunny? Huh?" Ahmaad gets in Sunny's face. He's so angry his dick gets hard. He started to tremble and tears welled in his eyes. Sunny started softening up. She felt every word he uttered and she felt a pain in her heart and a twinge in her pussy. Ahmaad's emotional state got to Sunny. She just wanted to make things right.

She wanted to make Ahmaad forget about everything and love on him one last time. Sunny grabs the sides of Ahmaad's face and he pulls away. She takes her ripped sundress off and lets it drop to the floor. She pulls Ahmaad's face again and this time he met her with less resistance.

"Baby I'm so sorry. I'm so fucking sorry. I don't want to lose you. You are the best thing that ever happened to me. Come here Ahmaad. I need you now." One tear fell from Ahmaad's right eye. He was weakened. He didn't want to fight. He didn't have it in him. He just wanted to love on Sunny. Sunny pulled him in and they kissed passionately. Biting each other lips, tongues caressing. Sunny pulled away and got on her knees. She kissed the tip of Ahmaad's dick and gave him head as if it was the last time she would ever suck a dick again. Ahmaad was about to explode in Sunny's mouth but she pulled his dick out once she started to feel the big vein down the shaft of his dick pulsate. Ahmaad was in ecstasy. Sunny got off her knees and guided Ahmaad to the bed. She straddled him and put the head of his dick at the entrance of her wet pussy. "I love you too, Ahmaad. Please forgive me." Sunny rammed Ahmaad's hard dick inside of her soaking wet center. They both let out sensual whales and moans.

Sunny rode Ahmaad like a wild bull. He couldn't last two minutes before his nut exploded inside Sunny's pussy. They both tried to catch their breath as sunny laid on his chest with his semi hard dick still nestled inside her walls. "What am I going to do with you woman?" Ahmaad whispered to Sunny; holding on to her for dear life. Sunny didn't respond. She just caressed his face until he fell asleep. Sunny eased out of the bed. Got dressed and looked at Ahmaad before creeping out of his apartment... for the last time.

Sunny couldn't stop the tears on her drive home down I-94 west. She could barely see thru the tears. She prayed she would make it to the Middlebelt exit without incident. Sunny felt lost, confused, angry, and mad at God, herself and definitely Ezra. "That muthafucka fucked up my life since day one. Why is this happening to me?

Why now? FUCK!!!!!!" It was nothing short of luck Sunny didn't get stopped by the police. Her speed topped out at 100mph. In a haze she made it home only to be met by Ezra parked in front of her house. Sunny felt flushed. She didn't know what to do so she braked and was parked in the middle of the street just before her driveway. She looked down at her ripped sundress and her just freshly fucked hair and she thought to herself, "fuck no. There's no way I can let him see me like this and expect to live." Sunny drove off. The minute she hit the corner her cell phone rings and of course it's Ezra.

"Hello." Sunny answers dryly. "Why in the hell did you stop and drive off when you know I'm sitting in front of your house waiting for you?" "Ezra, just because I'm pregnant with your baby doesn't give you the right to pop up whenever you fucking feel like it. A phone call would've been nice. We haven't spoken in 2 months and now you think you can just pop up on me like you trying to catch me in some bullshit or something.

You're not my man you're Shalisha's man. Let's not forget that. Just go home and I will call you tomorrow. I'm just not in the mood to be dealing with this shit." Sunny was hoping he fell for this act she was putting on. And it worked. "You are something else girl. Alright cool. I'll see you tomorrow. But you need to get home. My baby needs rest. Later." Ezra ends the call. Sunny is so relieved she dodged the biggest bullet in her life to date. She felt a sense of happiness and elation when Ezra said his baby needed rest. She couldn't help but smile. As she turned down her street she saw Ezra's tail lights.

Sunny was restless all night. She had so much on her heart. She felt so conflicted between Ezra and Ahmaad, but she wanted to give Ezra another chance. She wanted her baby to have both parents. She wanted the white picket fence, 2.5 kids, husband and dog and she always saw this dream with Ezra. She couldn't deny the feelings she had for Ahmaad though. He was everything she wished Ezra could be; A real man.

You have mail

"This nigga don't waste no time. It's too early to be texting. Damn, Ezra is anxious." Thought Sunny.

> *I woke up and you were gone. No goodbye no anything. Just, a cold bed. I understand why Sunny. I only want the best for you. You've made your decision and I WILL respect it. My heart will heal in time. If you ever need anything I will always be here for you. Love still, Ahmaad*

Sunny's heart sank. She felt fucked up and relieved at the same time. She was relieved Ahmaad wasn't making this situation harder than it already is, but the young immature part of Sunny wanted Ahmaad to act an asshole and fight for his woman. Despite her carrying another mans seed. She sat up in her bed and shed a few tears. Dried her face and took a long bath.

12

boom boom boom Sunny's mom

knocked on the bathroom door and walked right

in startling Sunny. "Mom!" Sunny yelled in an

annoyed tone. "Girl shut up. You pregnant ain't

you? Whose is it Sunny?" Sunny dropped her

head as low as she could. Ashamed,

embarrassed and disappointed. She sat in

silence for what seemed an eternity. She

managed to mutter, "It's Ezra's." Sunny's

mother face fell. She stood still and stared at

Sunny with a look of utter disappointment and disgust. A look Sunny has NEVER seen on her mother's face.

Her mother walked out of the bathroom and returned immediately with a pen and check book in hand. She wrote on one of her checks and ripped it out of the book. "Take this blank check. Make an appointment this week to get rid of it. Find out how much the procedure is and fill out the rest of the check." Sunny's mom sat the check down on the bathroom vanity and closed the door behind her. Sunny couldn't believe what just happened. All she wanted was to cry on her mother's shoulder. Get a hug and words of wisdom and encouragement. She wanted her mom to tell her she was going to support her decisions.

Sunny's emotions turned to anger. She couldn't believe her mom could be so cold and callus. She got out of the tub dried off and threw her robe on. She went into her mother's room and politely sat the check on the night stand. "I don't need your got damn check. I need a mother!" Sunny storms out of her mother's room and slams her bedroom door and starts packing an overnight bag. She was going to Ezra's for a few days until she cooled off and figured out her next move. She knew she couldn't stay with her mother because she wouldn't allow it. Sunny's mother loathed Ezra. Every mother's worst nightmare for their daughter. Sunny understood why she hated her child's father but she didn't understand why her mother couldn't show sympathy and empathy for her daughter. Sunny had to leave and think of a master plan.

Without calling or texting Sunny arrives at Ezra's doorstep with bags in tow. "I'm doing the same shit I told his ass not to do. Oh well, I'm the pregnant one. He better open up this damn door." Sunny thinks to herself out loud as she rings Ezra's doorbell. He opens the door and he looks like he just woke up. Sleep still in his eyes. "Sunny what are you doing here so early? What's up with the bags?" Sunny became agitated. "So are you going to let me in or what? Move Ezra It's cold!" Ezra is hesitant but he steps aside and lets Sunny in.

Sunny heads for the basement where Ezra's room is, but before she can make it down the first step he grabs her arm. "Sun wait. Shalisha is here." Sunny snatches her arm away. "Oh that's perfect. Let's tell her the good news. Shalisha! Shalisha wake up boo boo kitty!" Sunny jogs down the steps in a hurry to get to Shalisha. Ezra is on her heels calling her name through gritted teeth as to not cause a scene in his grandmother's house on a Sunday morning. Ezra tries holding Sunny back but there's no use; he lets her go. Sunny kicks open Ezra's bedroom door with her foot and Shalisha sits straight up in the bed; asshole naked.

"What the fuck E? Why in the fuck is she here?" Shalisha yells. "Oh your *man* didn't tell you we're having a baby? Yeah well I'm pregnant with his first born. And I have you to thank. The night you ate my pussy and his butthole is when he put his seed inside me. So thanks girl, but you can get your shit and get the fuck out now."

Sunny stands at the foot of the bed with her arms folded waiting on Shalisha to do as she ordered. "E, are you just going to stand there and let this shit fly?" Shalisha pleads to Ezra. "Bitch, what the fuck you think he's going to do? Side with you? Put you above me? You are one silly bitch!" Sunny sees Shalisha's panties and bra on the floor so she grabs them and throws them outside the room. She sees her clothes on the chair and she throws them on the floor outside the room. "Bitch, get dressed. He'll call you when he needs the shit cleaned off his ass crack." Ezra gets frustrated with Sunny, "Sunny, chill out bro. You doing too much. She's leaving, damn."

Shalisha snatches the covers off her body, stands up and lets them both look at her 5'4"

145 lbs. frame. She takes her time and walks out of the room. She doubles back and kisses Ezra on the lips and says, "Call me when this shit is over." Sunny smacks Shalisha on the ass with all of her strength. Shalisha stumbles, almost falling face first. "He will, bitch." Shalisha gathered her clothes and got dressed within 30 seconds flat and stormed out of the house. Ezra leaned against his wall and shook his head at Sunny. "What am I going to do with you girl." Sunny rolls her eyes and says, "First you can change these stanking ass sheets. Please and thank you." Ezra changes his sheets; he knew better than to challenge Sunny when she's in this state. While he's cleaning his room Sunny explains everything that happened between her and her mom. "Fuck your mama. You can stay here until we get our own crib.

She never liked me anyway so fuck her. We're going to be alright. Don't even let that shit get to you. I got you. All we need is each other flat the fuck out." Ezra says with his chest sticking out.

Sunny is 5 months pregnant and is really starting to show. She can't fit anything anymore. She and Ezra are still living in his grandmother's basement, but their relationship seems to be improving. Sunny lays in bed on her lap top trying to finish her final exam online just before the Christmas break. She hears Ezra coming inside the house. He comes into their room bearing gifts wearing a Santa Clause hat. "ho ho ho Mama Clause! Look what daddy got you for being a good girl."

Ezra has at least 10 different shopping bags. He loved lacing Sunny. It made him feel like a man. Made him feel proud and feel like a provider. Sunny starts squealing like a school girl. "Oooh daddy daddy daddy lemme see!! I have been a good girl! Ezra you went crazy! Christmas isn't for another two weeks!" Ezra, "You deserve Christmas everyday Sun. Straight up. Plus, I'm getting tired of you squeezing into these tight ass jeans cutting off my baby airway. So I had to get you together." Sunny burst into a laughing fit. "Shut up asshole! You better still love me with all of this juiciness I'm gaining." Ezra says, "I love you more juicier. That's why I can't keep my mouth off your pussy. Now hurry up and try your new gear on so I can eat on my pussy."

Ezra bought Sunny an entire new maternity wardrobe. Sunny figured he took his sister with him because he doesn't know the first thing about maternity clothes or what's fashionable. Things like this that Ezra did for Sunny made her feel as if everything would be ok. He would provide for her and their child. "Daddy, thank you so much. I really appreciate you taking care of me. Of us...I love you so fucking much. We're going to be alright. I just know it!"

Ezra looked at Sunny with pride and love. I told you Sun...I got us. I'm going to get a legit job and leave this street shit behind before my son gets here. I have to be the example you know." Sunny exclaims. "Son? You mean daughter...the world doesn't need another Ezra running around here. Ezra starts tickling Sunny after that snide remark. Things really couldn't be better for the two of them.

Considering everything that's transpired between them, one would never think they would be in a good space together as a couple.

13

Sunny is finally finished with her final exam. She has to go to campus to turn in her report to her professor and she can put this semester in the books. One more step closer to her dreams of becoming an RN. It's a beautiful winter's day driving down I-94 East, with fresh snow on the asphalt. Sunny always loved the snow. She pulls into the campus parking lot and she sees Ahmaad for the first time since she left him cold in his apartment 3 months ago.

Word around campus was he took a semester off after everything that happened between them. Sunny's body couldn't help but respond to seeing Ahmaad. Her stomach dropped and her pussy started thumping. Sunny thought to herself, "bitch, get your pregnant ass together. Please God don't let him see me." Sunny tries to sink down in her seat but Ahmaad spots her. He stood still for what seemed an eternity. He gave Sunny a smirk and mouthed "it's good to see you." He got in his car and drove off.

Sunny felt relieved but slighted that he didn't want to see her or speak to her. This made her want to reach out to him even more; to see if he'd really gotten over her. Sunny, then, suddenly felt a strong flutter in her belly. "Oh my god! My baby! Hi mamas baby!" Sunny just chuckled to herself because even her baby had more sense than she... "You really are mommies saving grace aren't you pumpkin."

Sunny turns in her report to her professor. Talks to a couple students who are shocked to finally notice her growing belly. Sunny is really proud to show off her growing bump. She loves talking about her baby to anyone who asks her due date. She loves all of the attention. Upon walking back to her car she sees a white piece of paper stuck to her windshield. "Just great! A fucking ticket on Christmas." She reads the white note and it simply reads, "Hungry?" Sunny is totally confused. She looks around and pulling in behind her car is Ahmaad. "Hey you...lunch, my treat?"

"Sure...why not. Hudson Café sounds good to me. I'll follow you." Sunny is in shock. She gets in her car and starts to squeal through her closed mouth. "I knew I still had it going on! Oh my God, what is he going to say? What if he curses me out? What if E, finds out? Oh my God Jesus be a fence of protection around my foolishness. I just need to know what he has to say to me after everything I did to him. The hostess seats Ahmaad and Sunny in a booth near the rear of the café. It's really busy but the booth gives them just enough privacy to have an intimate conversation. "You look well Sunny. You're glowing. Pregnancy looks good on you." Sunny blushes and thanks him for the compliment. "I just really wanted to catch up with you. Make sure everything was good for you. Even after the way things ended between you and I, I still care about your well-being. Soooo, how are you doing Sunny?"

Sunny cheeks are turning red. She's blushing and she can't hide her excitement. She's never been good at hiding her true feelings. "I am good Ahmaad. My baby is due in May, school is going well. Ezra and I are working things out for the sake of our baby. I can't really complain about much. I'm just trying to grow up a little bit you know. Prepare for this baby and get my degree you know. How are things with you?" Ahmaad isn't good at hiding his emotions either. He looks a bit disappointed but he tries to hide it with a weird grin. Like a, 'I'm so happy for you but I'm not really grin.' "That's great, Sunny. I'm glad to hear all is well. I'm doing ok. I took a semester off to clear my head but I'm back. Working at JNAP full time, plus school so, I don't have much time for anything or anyone, you know? But I'm good. I'm just in grind mode. My eyes are on the prize."

The food arrives and there's an uncomfortable silence between the two of them. Sunny feels like she's being fake with pleasantries. She can't hold back what she wants to say. "Ahmaad, I still think about you often. I was falling for you, Hard. And I feel fucked up the way I ended things between you and I. I just need you to know, if I weren't pregnant I believe things would be very different. I'm just trying to do what I think is best for this baby. But just know I will never forget you and you will always be the one whom I let get away."

Ahmaad says nothing. He just stares at Sunny. His stare is so intense it's as if he is staring into her soul. Sunny feels uncomfortable so she shifts in her seat, picks up her knife and fork, "well let's not let this food get cold." She felt as if she stepped out of line. Why does she always play with fire? Why can't she learn to control her mouth and pussy? Why?

"Sunny, you were the one who got away. I wish you would've given us a chance. My love for you is real. I would've and still will take care of you and your baby. I won't ever get over you. My one true love. But, I want you to know I love you enough to let you go. It's just good to see you doing well. Listen, I can't front. I thought I could handle this but I can't." Ahmaad gets his wallet out and pulls out a hundred dollar bill.

"This should cover lunch. Be good Sunny. I love you. Always." He gets up from the table and leaves Sunny looking clueless. She doesn't know what just happened. She's confused, angry, embarrassed and turned on. She grabs her purse and runs after Ahmaad in hopes of catching him. She sees him getting inside his car across the street from the café. " Ahmaad, wait!!" Sunny yells after him. Ahmaad stands in front of his car door looking as if his heart is racing a million miles a second. Sunny walks over to him, "How dare you embarrass me like that. You invite me to lunch, unload this shit on me and just leave me in the café alone? You don't even give me a chance to respond to anything you've said. Why would you even ask me to lunch? Why even turn around and leave the note on my car, huh? I mean what the fuck

Ah..." Ahmaad grabs Sunny's face and kisses

her passionately. Sunny kisses him back.

"Follow me to my house, Sunny." Sunny stares

at Ahmaad but doesn't move. She's speechless.

"Sunny, I need you to follow me to my house.

Come on." Ahmaad grabs Sunny's hand and

walks her to her car. "I live in Redford now so

stay close behind me. I don't want you to get

lost." Sunny whispers ok.

Sunny is in utter disbelief. "What the fuck

am I doing? I can't do this? I'm pregnant with

Ezra's baby for God's sake! What am I doing?

This is so trifling and foul. I can't. I just can't do

this to E!" Sunny is battling with her desires and

her conscience. She knows what she needs to

do but what she wants to do seem to be taking

over because she hasn't turned her car around

yet. Ahmaad pulls into his driveway and his home is beautiful. She pulls behind him and parks. "Come on Sunny. No pressure, okay? I just want to talk to you in private." Sunny follows behind Ahmaad. His home is just as beautiful on the inside but it's bare. He has a tv, a couch and a bed in his bedroom that's it. "Ahmaad why am I here? I'm pregnant with another man's baby Ahmaad. I mean what the fuck am I doing here?"

"Sunny sit down. Relax. I don't want you to think. I want you to just sit and talk to me. Just enjoy being in the moment. I don't want you to do anything you will regret or anything that is making you uncomfortable. So if you feel as if you shouldn't be here AND you don't want to be here, please allow me to walk you to your car. If you want to be here please have a seat and let me get you some ice water or some juice. We have to keep you and baby hydrated. Is that ok? Can I fix you both a glass of cran-apple juice?" Sunny smirks and giggles. She thought it was cute he was referencing her and the baby. "Yeah...I'd like...I mean we'd like that very much." Ahmaad fixes her some juice and they sit down and laugh and talk about everything that's happened in the past 3 months. He rubs her feet and legs while laughing at Sunny's impersonation of one of the professors at Wayne State.

"This was really nice. I'm glad I came by Ahmaad. Thank you for being a gentleman and taking care of me. You are something rare. Whoever marries you is one lucky bitch and I hate her." Sunny giggles but she's sincere and Ahmaad knows it. "I think it's time for me to go before I rape you or something. Must be something in the cran-apple juice. Can I use your restroom?" "First door on the left baby girl." Says Ahmaad. Sunny uses the bathroom and she can't help but to snoop around. She opens the medicine cabinet and she sees their picture. The picture they took on the night the first time they made love. Sunny starts to cry. One, because she's pregnant; but, two because she realizes Ahmaad really is in love with her. She is flooded with so many thoughts and emotions. She knows she has to get out of there and go home. She tries to straighten her face and dry her eyes so Ahmaad wouldn't know she was crying and snooping in his bathroom. She gives herself and pep talk and opens the door.

Ahmaad is standing in front of her. "Don't leave me Sunny. Not yet." Ahmaad pulls Sunny into his arms and kisses her. "Ahmaad, I can't. I can't do this." Sunny says...."Shhh stop talking Sunny. Stop thinking. Turn off your mind. Open your heart one last time and let me in." Sunny eyes well up and she can't control herself any longer. She grabs Ahmaad and kisses him passionately. He picks her up and carries her to his bedroom. He gently lays her in his bed and kisses her tears off her cheeks. "Don't cry my love. Don't cry." Ahmaad whispers to Sunny. He undresses Sunny so gently as if she were a priceless doll. He stops and stares at her protruding belly. "I can't help but wish this baby was mine. You are the most beautiful pregnant woman I've ever seen. Please, stand up Sunny. Let me take you in." Ahmaad requested. Sunny does what she's asked to do and Ahmaad stares at her body very intensely. She can't help but notice his dick print growing inside his jeans. She gets wet, instantly. Ahmaad is filled with lust. He is intoxicated by Sunny's body. Her swollen breast and protruding nipples make Ahmaad's dick grow. Sunny's hips have spread as to accommodate her growing baby. Her ass is ripe and supple. Her skin is glowing like fresh honey from a comb. Her hair luscious thick and flowing down her back.

He's never looked at a pregnant woman sexually until Sunny. Sunny has changed the game. Ahmaad couldn't hold back any longer. He walks over to Sunny, "May I kiss you here?" He asks... Sunny's breathing is slightly labored.

She whispers, "yes." Ahmaad kisses Sunny on her neck. One of her erogenous zones. She lets out a low moan. Sunny can't deny what her body wants. She gives in to her fleshly desires. "Ahmaad, I've missed your touch. I've missed you Ahmaad. Fuck, I've missed you. Ahhhh" Sunny moans and groans lustfully.

Ahmaad traces every inch of Sunny's skin with his tongue. His dick is as hard as a steel pipe. He can't wait another second. He needs to be inside Sunny's walls. "Let me inside my pussy Sun. Let me in now. I need to feel you on my dick, Sun." Sunny opens her legs wide. She takes her hand and opens her pussy lips, exposing her swollen clitoris. It's as if she just opened a seashell with a beautiful shiny wet pearl inside. She uses her index and middle fingers and starts making circles on her clit. Ahmaad is so turned on he has pre-cum dripping down the shaft of his dick. Ahmaad grabs Sunny's hands and sucks her pussy juice off her fingers. He knows this drives her wild. "Fuck me now Ahmaad. Fuck me please! Don't make me beg. I can't take it." Ahmaad knew he had her right where he wanted her. He gets on his knees and dives into her sweet center head first. He sucks on her clit to draw it outside of the hood even more. He wants it to be fully exposed and swollen. He encircles her clit with his tongue and goes back to sucking. Circles, suck, circles, suck, circles. "Ahmaad im going to cum so hard.

Make me cum all over your face Ahmaad. You better make me cum hard. Oh fuck!

Fuuuuuuckkkkkk!! Oh god Ahmaad! This feels

so good. Please don't stop baby! Don't stop!"

Sunny screams out in pure ecstasy. Ahmaad

goes in for his finishing move. He brings out the

snake. He starts flicking his tongue like a

reptile. A snake. He feels Sunny's clit swelling

up and pulsating. He knows she's going to

climax any second so he dares not move from

this position. Her legs stiffen, belly tightens and

she arches her back.

Ahmaad is so turned on by making Sunny

climax, the big vein running down the shaft of

his cock starts to pulsate. He's in euphoria.

They explode orgasmically in harmony. Ahmaad

takes his hand and wipes Sunny's nectar from

his beard and he licks it off his hand. He takes

the same hand and strokes all 9 inches of his

manhood all while never taking his eyes off of her. She is still trembling from her orgasm. Ahmaad leans into her ear, "I'm going to fuck you until you love me." Ahmaad takes his dick and rubs the head against Sunny's red, swollen, pulsating clit. He uses the head of his dick to spread her juices around; making the circles slippery and more pleasurable. Circles, slap, circles, slap; as he uses the head of his dick like a masseuse on her pussy.

Ahmaad slides the first two inches inside of Sunny's soaking wet center and he slides it out. He slides it back in this time 3 inches and slides it out. Driving Sunny wild. He Slides all 9 inches in ever so gently while Sunny screams in ecstasy. He slowly thrust his hips, driving his dick as deep as he could inside of her warm creamy mound, all the while being careful not to hurt her bulging belly filled with Ezra's child.

He looks at Sunny's face, painted with lust and pleasure. Ahmaad picks up his speed as he feels his nut sack tightening and his shaft thumping. He looks at her belly and can't help but feel anger and resentment. He thrusts harder. And harder. "Ahhh fuck. Ouch baby, wait." Sunny says while wincing in discomfort. Ahmaad's face turns red and his brows furrow. He thrust harder and faster pinning her hands behind her head so she can't move. "Ahmaad you're hurting me! Owww!!" Sunny is yelping. "Im about to cum! I'm cumming! Ahhhhhhhhhhhhh!!!!!!!!" Ahmaad lets out an animalistic growl as he unloads his semen inside Sunny's walls.

Sunny pushes Ahmaad off her. She feels violated. This awkward silence fills the room. Sunny instantly regrets everything. She grabs her clothes and goes to the bathroom. Ahmaad doesn't budge. He is silent. Sitting on the side of his bed. Sunny turns on the water to muffle her cries. "Why did I do this? Why? What is wrong with me? I gotta get out of here"

She thought to herself as she cleaned herself up and got dressed. She goes back into the room to grab her purse and Ahmaad isn't there. He's in the kitchen shirtless with his basketball shorts on staring out of the window. "Ahmaad, I'm going to go. I guess this is goodbye. This is the closure you were looking for I suppose. Take care of yourself." Sunny makes a b line for the door and she hears Ahmaad sniffle. "I know he isn't crying" she thought. She walks over to him and he turns his head. "Man, just go. Good luck with your kid and life. I apologize for hurting you."

Sunny grabs his face and sees the tears falling down his face. His eyes blood red. "Ahmaad, talk to me. Please, what's wrong? What was that about?" Ahmaad pulls his face away from her grasp. "Sunny, it just hit me you're pregnant with a hoe ass nigga baby and you actually left me for him. So I guess I got a little lost in my feelings. But you're right I guess this is the closure I needed. Just leave Sunny. I can't even look at you, bro. Just go." Sunny is flooded with emotions.

Before she could utter a word her hand went across Ahmaads face with all of her might.

"Fuck you, Ahmaad! Fuck you for using me! I never want to see you again!" Ahmaad is stunned. Sunny runs to her car. She's a wreck, bawling her eyes out. She feels nauseous and vomits in Ahmaads lawn. Ahmaad runs after her and pulls her hair back while she throws up. "Sunny, calm down. Don't upset the baby okay, Sun? Please calm down. I'm so sorry Sun. I'm sorry baby, don't upset yourself. Come back inside Sunny. Please?" Ahmaad holds Sunny up and brings her back inside his house. He closes the door and sits her down on his sofa. He grabs a wash cloth and wets it with warm water, kneels down and washes Sunny's face. "I didn't mean to upset you like this Sunny. I'm just, so hurt. I am madly in love with you Sunny. And I don't know what to do about it. I don't know what to do Sunny, but the last thing I want to do is hurt you. Please forgive me babygirl?" Sunny calms down and the tears stop. She's so confused and tormented. She can't help but to become soft again. She knows everything Ahmaad is saying is genuine and from the heart.

She feels as if she should be with Ahmaad. She knows she could have the life she wants with him. But the way he feels about her, she feels for Ezra. "I forgive you Ahmaad. You really hurt me. I understand it though. I'm really fucked up right now Ahmaad. Like, real shit. I'm pregnant with another man's baby and I just fucked you. I love him and I love you. I'm fucking pregnant Ahmaad. Do you see my fucking belly! Look at my belly! This baby isn't yours Ahmaad! And I let you fuck me! What kind of woman am I?" Sunny starts to cry again.

"You're a woman in love Sunny. This doesn't make you less of a woman or mother. It makes you human and shit happens. You can't help how you feel. You can't help what you want. But, I need to know right now today...Do you see a future with me? Me, you and the baby. Can you see it? Can you see us living happily ever after?" Ahmaad puts his hands on Sunny's belly and rubs it. "I will love and raise this baby as my own, because I love you and anything that comes from you. Anything that's apart of you. Anything that you create. Anything that has an essence of you I will always love and cherish. Do you understand that?" Sunny is speechless. All she can do is shake her head yes, but she really doesn't understand the depths of what Ahmaad is professing to her.

This man will do anything for her and will love her until his dying day. This is something she's longed for since she's been a little girl. Unconditional love from a man, But it's not from who she wants. She doesn't have the heart to tell Ahmaad. She can't stand to hurt him yet again. "Will you wait for me Ahmaad? I just need some time to figure everything out. Will you wait for me?" Sunny asks... "I will wait for you Sun. Until I can't wait anymore. I'm here, okay? I am here Sunny." Sunny grabs Ahmaad and they embrace each other on the couch until they both fell asleep in each other's arms.

14

Chirp! Chirp! Chirp! Sunny wakes up to hear her phones notifications going off. It's midnight and Ezra has called her over 20 times. "Shit! Shit! Shit! Ahmaad, I gotta go. Baby I gotta go home." Sunny kisses Ahmaad goodbye. Ahmaad, halfway asleep, "Why you gotta go bae? Just stay the night." Sunny looks at him like come on you know better. " Ahmaad I live with Ezra. I can't do that. Remember you said you would give me some time. I will call you tomorrow."

Sunny pulls off and she's quickly thinking
of an excuse to give Ezra as to why she's been
gone all this time and ignored all of his calls.
She calls Tyra. "Hey pumpkin what ya doing?
So listen I need you to cover for me okay. I was
with you all day we went to eat at Sevas and I
fell asleep at your crib, okay?" Tyra says, "Bitch
what have you gotten your PREGNANT ass into
now? Don't have me kill Ezra when he puts his
hands on you again. But anyway I got you. I
gotta go, bye bitch." Tyra hangs up. Sunny
misses her friend. She knows she hasn't been a
good friend to Tyra because she hasn't been
around much. She's making a point to spend
some time with her. Now, on to making the
dreaded call to Ezra.

"Sunny where in the fuck are you?" Ezra

asked very calmly. It was a scary calm. "Oh my god baby I'm so fucking sorry. I fell asleep over Tyra's. After school I went over there and we went to grab a bite to eat came back to her crib to go over these term papers and my pregnant ass passed out. This baby got me so exhausted." Sunny almost believed the lie her damn self. "I drove past Tyra's and your car wasn't there. I expect you to pull up within the next ten minutes." Click.

Sunny pulls up at Ezra's. Her stomach is in knots. Palms sweaty, her breathing is labored. Nervous is an understatement. Sunny is afraid. The house is dark. Ezra's grandmothers TV is on in her room but she is sound asleep. She goes downstairs where Ezra is sitting in the dark smoking a blunt. "Hey baby, why are you sitting in the dark?" Sunny asks; acting as if she didn't just hop off another man's dick. Ezra doesn't respond. He continues to take a long drag from his blunt. "Really bae? Since you wanna do drive-by's and act crazy you should've called Tyra and she would've told you the deal. She took my car to go see her dude while I was asleep. I mean where else do you think I would be Ezra? You don't trust me for shit. This is getting real old and tired. I'm going to bed. I hope you will join me."

Sunny is praying her lie is bought. She goes into their room and starts to undress. Ezra comes behind her and places his large hand around her neck. He has a firm grip. Firm enough to confuse Sunny. She's not sure if he's upset or wants to fuck. "I've been worried sick about you all day. You have to be more mindful of what you're doing and who you're doing it with while you have my baby inside you." Ezra whispered into Sunny's ear. Sunny didn't utter a word. She didn't understand what Ezra meant by that. She was playing it cool because she didn't know what he was going to do next. She felt as if he knew somehow. As if he could smell Ahmaad's sweat and semen on her.

Ezra releases his grip on Sunny's neck and unsnaps her bra; Watching her full breast fall slightly. He motions for her to pull her panties down. She obliges. "Slowly. Take them off slowly." Ezra demands. Sunny is experiencing de ja vue. She just undressed for another man in the same manner less than 6 hours ago. Sunny knew she had to go along with anything

Ezra asked of her. She knew better than to let on something was up.

Ezra stares at Sunny long and hard. As if he sees thru her. Sees all of her dirty secrets. All of her lies. His eyes turn cold yet he is silent. He takes off his clothes. Ezra's member is fully erect. His veins in his arms and neck are bulging. He's breathing faster than usual. "Lie down Sunny." Sunny is too afraid to object. She lies down and she starts to shake because Ezra starts to sniff her like a dog. He sniffs her neck, behind her ears, her mouth, her breast, her pubic hairs, her inner thighs, behind her knees, her buttocks. He grabs her right leg and puts it on his shoulder. He never breaks eye contact with Sunny.

He grabs his dick and guides it inside

Sunny's freshly fucked pussy. He guides it in slowly and says, "Hmm" He slowly guides his dick out and he glides right back in and says, "Hmm" again. Ezra bends down and whispers in Sunny's ear, "Your pussy used to curve to my dick until today, whore." Sunny tries to get up but Ezra pushes her back down. "Get the fuck off me! Get off me now!" Sunny is screaming. "Baby calm down, CALM DOWN! I'm just bullshitting with you daaaamn!" Ezra says to Sunny while laughing uncontrollably. Sunny is relieved yet leery. "Get off me E. What the hell is wrong with you? That ain't funny I can't believe you." Ezra is still laughing, "Baby come here. Aww lil mama you deserved it. You had me worried all night about you and my son. Give me some sugar." Sunny is still shaking but she gives Ezra a kiss. "Ok now goodnight I'm

still tired. You had me going asshole." Sunny
says with relief.

Today is the day Sunny and Ezra finds out
the sex of their baby. They couldn't be more
excited. "I know it's a boy. I can feel it. Doc how
much you wanna bet we having a boy?" Ezra
says to the ultrasound technician: proudly and
with much excitement. The technician just
laughs and says, "Well sir, I would advise you to
play lotto today because you're definitely having
a baby boy." "Yeah ! Yeah! I told you! Yeah!
Yeah! That's my boy! Hey man man! Hey daddy's
boy! Daddy can't wait to see you!" Ezra shouts
with excitement and Sunny just lies silently on
the table while tears stream down the sides of
her face. She's happy and in turmoil at the
same time.

She can't stop thinking about Ahmaad. She hasn't spoken to him since their last encounter two weeks ago. She's in love with Ezra but she knows he isn't what she needs. He is a drug dealer, no education, and no security blanket for her or their baby. Let's not forget about his violent streak. Sunny's mom always told her once an abuser always an abuser. The night she was with Ahmaad she was terrified of Ezra hurting her physically. She just realized she's actually afraid of him and what he's capable of doing to her. So many thoughts flood into her mind and she can't hide it. "Sunny baby where are you? You hear that? You gave me my first son! Sunny, thank you. Thank you for loving me. Thank you for my son Sunny. I love you so fucking much Sun."

Ezra starts to cry tears of Joy as he gets on one knee and cradles Sunny's belly. "You two are such a treat! But, hang on papa I have to get some measurements and make sure everything is good in there." Ezra scoots up to Sunny's face and kisses her over and over while professing his love for her. He reaches in his jacket pocket and pulls out a ring box. The ultrasound technician stops taking measurements. Sunny's eyes are as big as half dollars. "Marry me Sunny. I told you, I was going to make you my wife. Marry a real nigga Sun. I will die protecting yall and providing for yall."

Sunny is in shock. "Of course I'll marry you E. Oh my God I can't believe you! This ring is beautiful. Put it on me now baby. I love you daddy." The newly engaged couple embrace and the technician is in tears, "Congratulations you two! This is a first for me." "Us too" Ezra and Sunny say in unison. Sunny was happy on the surface but on the inside she was still drowning in her own hell that she created.

On the ride home, Ezra was glued to his phone telling everyone he knew they were having a baby boy. Sunny looked down at her ring and belly the entire ride home. Ezra notices when they pulled into the driveway. "What's up with you Sun? You in shock or something?" Sunny looks at him and smiles but her eyes tell a different story. "I don't know E. Everything just seems so real now. I guess everything has hit me. We're really having a baby and we're getting married. This is a lot. You sure you ready for all this? You want to settle down with me for life?" Ezra looks at Sunny puzzled. "If I didn't know any better I would say you the one who not ready Sunny. You tripping. Come on lets tell grandma the news."

Ezra's grandmother is over the moon about the news of the baby and more excited about the engagement. She pulls out her old pictures of her wedding to her 2nd husband. Her true love she says. She talks wedding talk for what seemed like hours while all Sunny could do was think how can she get away to see Ahmaad. "Granny you have some great ideas. I'm gonna go to my mom's house, we have to continue this later. I love you granny." Sunny had to get out of their before she lost the little bit of mind she had left. "Babe, I'm going over my moms and

Tyras house I'll be back later on." Sunny yells

downstairs to Ezra. "Alright, don't do what you

did the last time you went over Tyra's. Answer

your damn phone. Wife." Sunny giggles and

says "Yes, Husband." She felt nauseous.

Sunny gets in her car and starts to drive

towards Ahmaads. She calls him but he doesn't

answer. She decides to go over his house

anyway. She needed to talk to him and she

couldn't wait one more day. She would wait all

night for him if she had to. She calls Tyra and

uses her as a scapegoat again. Tyra sounds

annoyed but she agrees and hangs up in her

friends' ear once again. Showing her

disapproval. Sunny arrives at Ahmaads and she

sees his car in the driveway with another car

behind his. "Oh, so he has a bitch in his house,

that's why he doesn't want to answer." Sunny

mumbles to herself. She dials Ahmaad's

number again. No answer. Again. No answer.

"Fuck this. He has to talk to me now."

Sunny waddles to Ahmaad's door and

rings the doorbell. She hears footsteps. She

rings it again back to back this time. Ahmaad

answers the door shirtless with jeans on and the

top button is unbuttoned. "Sunny, what's going

on?" Sunny rolls her eyes as hard as she could,

"I need to talk to you about a situation. I see

you have company but this is urgent like a

muthafucka, muthafucka." Sunny says with as

much attitude as she can muster while crossing

her arms over her growing belly and tapping her

foot. "Come in Sun." Ahmaad opens the door

for Sunny. She walks in and sits on the couch.

Marvin Gaye is crooning in the background. Candles and incense are burning. He goes into his bedroom and closes the door.

Five minutes later a flushed face angry Puerto Rican girl comes out of the room speaking in Spanish saying what sounds to be swear words. She looks at Sunny sitting on the couch. "Oh hell no you got a pregnant girlfriend? Nigga fuck you! Lose my number asshole! And good luck to you home girl you're gonna need it dealing with his lying ass." Ahmaad interrupts the Puerto Rican slut, "Don't you ever address her in your fucking life. Now please get the fuck out." Ahmaad slams the door in the girls face.

"I didn't mean to interrupt your little fuck session. My bad." Sunny states sarcastically.

Ahmaad rolls his eyes, "yes you did. I haven't heard from you in over two weeks. And you just pop up on a nigga. Talk." Ahmaad says irritated. "I told you I needed some time. I'm sorry it took two weeks but I didn't expect you to jump into a new relationship. I mean fuck. But who am I to question what you do. This was a mistake coming over here. I feel stupid as fuck. I don't know where to go. Who to talk to. You were the only person I could think of, the only one I wanted to talk to, okay. I haven't been able to stop thinking about you Ahmaad, alright. So I'm here. Fuck."

Sunny starts to cry. She's so overwhelmed with emotions she couldn't hold back. Ahmaad rubs her back and lets her get it out. When her sobbing subsided, he asks, "Is that what I think it is on your finger?" Sunny

looks down at her hand and says yes. "I had my

ultrasound today and when the tech said it's a

boy he proposed. And I said yes. I felt so fucked

up because all I kept thinking about was you.

You being at this doc appointment. You

proposing to me. Me having your son not his. I

don't know what the fuck to do. I'm so stressed

out I feel like I can't breathe. The night I came

home after being with you I thought he was

going to kill me. I'm legit terrified of the nigga

I'm having a baby with and supposedly

marrying. How does this make sense? How?

And why does he still sell dope and we're still

living in his grandmother's basement? I'm

supposed to bring my baby home to live in a got

damn basement? How is this my life? When he

fucks me I can't even cum if I don't think about

your dick inside me. Your hands touching me. What the fuck Ahmaad?!"

Sunny unloads everything she's been feeling the past two weeks unto Ahmaads lap. He never stops caressing her back. Letting her know he got her no matter what. Ahmaad gets up and takes Sunny's boots off. He starts to massage her feet. "Listen Sunny, I told you I would wait and I meant it. I'm not going to lie to you. I am a man and I have needs. I get lonely in this house. So I want you to know that I am seeing other women. But just as I did tonight I will drop anyone for you. Because I know who I want and what I want. What you need to do is turn your brain off. Relax. Stop thinking. And just breathe baby. You can't stress like this. You have to make some hard decisions only you can make. Pray on it and do what's in the best

interest of you and your son. I told you where I

stand. It will NEVER change. But right now I

need you here with me. And I need you to relax.

Most importantly I need you to take off that ring

while you're here with me."

Sunny takes off her 4 hour old

engagement ring and puts it inside her purse.

"That's better. Just relax baby girl. I got you. I

just want you to decompress and relax." Sunny

needed this attention, this escape. She just

melts into Ahmaads hands and couch and he

rubs her feet for an hour straight. She falls

asleep and he grabs a blanket and tucks her in.

He was even kind enough to take her phone out

of her purse and put it next to her head. He

didn't want to have to hurt this man if he put

hands on Sunny for not answering his call.

Sunny woke up an hour later feeling refreshed. She smelled spaghetti and it made her mouth water. She thought she should call Ezra to check in. "Hey babe me and Tyra downtown at the casino. Just wanted you to know. Love you." Sunny was relieved Ezra didn't answer the phone. She tip toed into the kitchen and hugged Ahmaad from behind. "Thank you Ahmaad. You give me peace." Sunny pulled Ahmaads face to hers and kissed him.

"Nothing to thank me for. It's my pleasure and my duty. Now cop a squat. I want you to feed that lil boy in there." Sunny felt pampered and spoiled. She loved every second of the attention. Ahmaad served Sunny dinner and after he placed her plate in front of her he grabbed her hands and said lets bless our food; and he prayed with her. For some reason this made her emotional.

She thought about her life as a wife, a mother and she envisions her child seeing her parents pray and treat each other in the same way she and Ahmaad treat each other. She kept thinking about the life she lives with Ezra. Never knowing if he's going to come home, selling drugs, always on the go, the constant traffic at the house, the women. She knew she couldn't bring her baby into that house with Ezra. This isn't the life she wants for neither her nor her son. Sunny wants Ahmaad. She wants the life he can give her and her baby.

"Dinner was amazing, Ahmaad. You made

my day. You took my worries and pain away for the moment. Thank you for taking care of me, of us. I just want you to know I really appreciate you. And...I love you Ahmaad. I fucking love you and I don't want to spend another night without you. I want to start my life with you. I'm done with Ezra. I'm done with lying to myself. My son deserves a normal healthy life. I can't give him that with Ezra. I kept using the fact that he is my son's father as an excuse to stay with him. No more, Ahmaad. If you'll still have me, I want you." Ahmaad stood still, stoic.

Sunny couldn't read him. She was starting to feel embarrassed. "Maybe he changed his mind" she thought. "So let's get your shit and move you in mama." Says Ahmaad. Sunny is relieved and starts giggling like a school girl. "Baby I'm not moving in. I need to find my own place. Live on my own. Be my own woman. I'm not trying to move out of my son's father's house to my boyfriend's house while I'm carrying his child. How does that look?"

Ahmaad sighed, "Sunny when are you going to learn no matter what it is you do with YOUR life; someone will always have something to say about how it looks, how it should be, what you should've done, if they were you what they would've done. You have to learn to stop caring what other people opinions are about you. This is your life. You make decisions for yourself and not based on what people will think. Do you think I give a fuck about what people will say about me being in a relationship with a pregnant woman? I don't give a fuck.

This is my life. I want what I want and I will

stop at nothing to get it. I want you. I need you.

I want your son. I want a life with the both of

you. Think about moving in. Don't tell me no

straight off. Just think about it. In the

meantime we have to get you out of this nigga

grandma's basement."

Sunny obliges to Ahmaads request. "I

need to figure out how I'm going to break the

news and get my stuff out of the house. I'm just

going to do it when he isn't home but I will tell

him what I need to tell him to end this shit. So

I'm gonna head home and start figuring this shit

out. Thank you for dinner baby. Will I see you

tomorrow?" Ahmaad smirks, "Yes you will.

Hopefully you will have all of your clothes with

you." Sunny grabs Ahmaad by the collar of his shirt and kisses him passionately. "I will see you tomorrow. I will have an overnight bag but that's probably it, sir."

On the drive home, reality starts to sink in. Sunny is in a panic. She needs to talk to a friend; her only friend, Tyra. Sunny finds herself on Tyra's doorstep. "Hi best friend. It's been too long." Sunny says to Tyra while stretching out her arms to welcome her into her bosom for a hug. Tyra hugs Sunny like she was a stranger, not her best friend. "Damn, bitch it's like that? I know I haven't been around much T, but please charge it to my head and not my heart. I've missed you. And I'm sorry for being a shitty friend. You forgive me?" Sunny starts to pout and of course Tyra couldn't hold a grudge.

"Yeah whatever bitch, I've missed you too. So what's been up?" Tyra says. "No, I want you to catch me up on what's been going on in your life. I need to get out of my head. So what's new?" Tyra catches sunny up on everything she has going on and she hits her with a bombshell. "Bitch what? A GIRLFRIEND? So you're gay now?" Sunny asks her friend. "No bitch I'm not gay I just like who and what I like and she just so happens to be a girl. I don't know Sun we have a good time together, she makes me feel like I'm the finest bitch walking and she makes me cum in 3.5 minutes. I mean you would be with her too, bitch. Don't act like you don't like your pussy ate from time to time." Tyra states matter of fact. "Ok this is about you not me. And I guess...as long as you're happy T. I mean really happy." Tyra looks at her friend and she sees through her and she is anything but happy. "Sunny, talk to me. What's going on with you? Is the baby ok?" Tyra asked her friend. Sunny unloads on her friend. She catches her up to everything that's been going on with her, Ahmaad and Ezra. She finds herself crying out of being overwhelmed and in total fear.

"Sun, you know Ezra won't let you go this easy. Are you prepared for whatever this fool will try? And why not just be single and date Ahmaad? Focus on school and your kid. You don't need to jump so fast girl. You're always jumping head first. Slow down baby you're moving too fast. I'm not trying to tell you what to do, I'm just concerned. Ain't nothing wrong with being by your damn self. You're only 19 Sunny, I mean what the fuck? And stop feeling like you owe somebody. You don't owe nobody

nothing but your damn self. So don't be with

Ahmaad out of obligation because you don't

want to hurt him. What's going to happen is

you're going to end up hurting yourself in the

end. I'm all for leaving Ezra because he ain't

about shit and he is a woman beater! But give

yourself some time Sun. You deserve it, you

know."

Tyra was speaking from the heart and

keeping it real with her confused friend. "This is

exactly what I needed. I love you T. Thank you

for being you. I got some shit to figure out so let

me get out of here. Let's do lunch next week?"

asks Sunny. "Yes bitch lets. It's on me since I

haven't had the chance to feed my baby yet.

You big as hell already by the way. But you sexy

though." The two friends laughed and embraced each other.

Sunny sat in Tyra's driveway in her car in deep thought. Her next stop was Ezra's. She didn't want to spend another night in that basement. Living what she felt was now a lie. She thought about calling her mom and asking to move back with her until she figured things out with Ahmaad. "Mama, I need to come back home." Sunny said to her mother over the phone.

"Sunny, you got a lot going on. Too much for this house. Now I will help you where I can but you can't come back here. You're grown now. Grow up. Good bye Sunny." Sunny's mother hung up the phone. She was in disbelief. She felt like that little 8 year old girl whose innocence was taken and no one there to protect her. She started sobbing. Sunny felt as if she wouldn't be in this situation if her parents protected her. If they supported her the way she felt a parent should support their child. She felt abandoned and alone. She just wanted love, support, comfort and a peace of mind. Ahmaad could give her all of this, she feels. She pulls herself together and goes home to Ezra's.

He isn't home and she decides to write him a letter and pack up all of her things.

Dear E, I can't do this. I'm sorry. I can't get over a lot of shit that's happened between us. I don't want to bring my baby home to your granny's basement. I want more out of life. We aren't meant to be. I will never keep your son away from you. I will let you know when the next doc apt is. Goodbye E - Sunny

Sunny leaves the engagement ring on top of the letter on his nightstand. She feels a sense of relief but also fear. She knows things won't end well. She just hopes by some miracle he will accept her choice and move on. Sunny's only option is to go back over to Ahmaad's.

15

"Welcome home baby." Ahmaad says as he opens his door to let Sunny in. "Is that all of your things in the car?" Sunny says yes and Ahmaad couldn't hold back his smile. He goes out to Sunny's car and brings all of her things inside. "Ahmaad I don't know what's going to happen next. I feel really afraid and unsure of a lot of things; except you. I'm putting everything into us Ahmaad. I don't have family, not many friends, I'm having this baby soon and all the odds in the world are against us. Just please be my friend no matter what. I don't want to lose that with you. It's really important to me, Ahmaad."

Ahmaad listens to Sunny intently, never taking his eyes off hers. "Sunny, you are my heart; my woman. You're carrying my step son. I will never allow anything to happen to either one of you. I love you woman. And I love this baby because of my love for you. I know what I'm taking on and I would take on 100 times more just to have you in my life. See, you don't understand something. I'm not afraid. I am a man. I am your man. I will take care of all of your needs, wants and desires. Just always remain loyal and true to me. I will do anything for you Sun. And I mean every word. I hope you feel my sincerity."

Sunny couldn't do anything except jump Ahmaads bones. They made love on the living room floor for what seemed like hours. Sunny released all of her frustrations, fears and worries unto Ahmaad's dick. They both collapsed in each other's arms. Sweating and panting. Sunny feels safe and secure in Ahmaads arms. She couldn't help but to fall into a deep slumber underneath his arm. Sunny is awakened by loud talking. She looks at the clock and it's 2:00 in the morning. Ahmaad put her in his bed but he isn't next to her.

"She's done fam. You need to let go and move on. Be there for your seed but Sunny wants no parts of you fam. You just got to eat that bro. Nigga you don't want problems with me. I don't do all this tough talking over the phone my nigga. Lick your wounds, calm down, get over your heartbreak and man up for you kid nigga. Don't call her phone unless it's about the baby after he gets here nigga." Sunny couldn't believe her ears. Ahmaad actually answered her phone and went off on Ezra. Ezra had no idea of any of this. Why would he do this? Why wouldn't he let me handle this? She gets out of the bed and puts on one of his t-shirts, and goes into the kitchen where he is standing.

"Ahmaad, what the fuck did you just do?" Sunny asks. "I handled it, that's what I did. This nigga calling you nonstop. I don't care what he just found out he gone know not to call you like this ever again. And this bitch ass nigga calling back?" Sunny snatches her phone. "Ahmaad stop it! Let me handle him. I wrote him a letter with his ring attached to it. He had

no idea of any of this. He didn't see this coming.

We were very much in love Ahmaad. He just

proposed to me. Why wouldn't you let me

handle this?! You're out of line! You just made

my life 100 times harder than it has to be!"

Sunny is frantic. She wants to hide under a

rock and never come out. Her phone is buzzing

nonstop. She knows Ezra is ready to kill. "You

know what; I need some air before I say

something I may regret. Deal with YOUR BABY

DADDY before I do." Ahmaad yells as he grabs

his coat and keys while walking out the door.

Sunny knows she has to answer Ezra's

phone call. "Hello" Sunny says as she hits the

answer button on her phone. "Sunny, where in

the fuck are you with my son? Is that even my

son you lying bitch? Who the fuck is this nigga Sunny? You been playing me this whole time bitch? You know what, whenever I see you I'm going to put my hands around your neck and squeeze until I feel your life slip from my hands you rat bitch." ***End call...***

Sunny was shaking. She didn't know what to do. And here she was alone, scared and confused. She didn't want to be in this house alone another second. She throws some clothes on and goes to Tyra's. Tyra's girlfriend was there but Sunny didn't care. She had no one else to turn to. So she told Tyra the latest. All Tyra could do was shake her head and her girlfriend was playing the PlayStation pretending not to listen. "Sunny you really did it this time. I don't know what to say. You need to protect yourself though. Get a PPO and a gun. You know how E gets down. I don't know what else to say girl." Tyra is disappointed in her friend and she isn't trying to hide it one bit.

Sunny is broken. "I'm going to go. Thanks for listening." Tyra grabs Sunny's hand. Sunny just chill. Sleep here tonight just so you can get a peace of mind and not deal with any one of them niggas until morning. You can't stress the baby; he's going to come out mean with grey hair." This made Sunny chuckle. "Thanks T. I will take you up on the offer. Oh and Ms. lady, I'm sorry I forgot your name. I'm sorry for taking up yall time. I was in a crisis." Sunny said to Tyra's lover. "Oh, it's cool ma. I hope everything gets better for you." Tyra's girlfriend reassures Sunny. "Come on you can sleep in my room.

Me and Joanie will sleep out here."

Tyra leads Sunny to her bedroom where she changes the sheets for her and tucks her in. She kisses Sunny on the head, "I love you Sun. Everything will work out and I got your back. Always." Sunny felt loved and comforted. "I love you T." Sunny tosses and turns. She tries to sleep but the birds outside are chirping and she hears moans coming from the living room. She tries to ignore it but she can't. Tyra is screaming out in ecstasy.

Sunny's curiosity got the best of her. She tip toes out of the room and peaks down the hall. She couldn't see anything so she creeps down the hall until she got a full visual. Joanie is going to work on Tyra's pussy. Tyra's legs are pushed back behind her head like a pretzel and

Joanie is eating her pussy like she's about to

walk the green mile. Sunny is getting turned on.

Before she realizes her hand is rubbing her

nipples. Tyra looks up and sees Sunny. She

tells Sunny to come here with her finger. Sunny

eyes got really big and she shook her head no.

"Sunny, come here. Please?" Tyra says. Joanie

lifts her head from Tyra's pussy with her face

shining like a glazed donut from Tyra's nectar.

Sunny slowly walks over to the two. Tyra grabs

Sunny's hand and motions for her to sit on the

couch. Joanie gets up and sits against the wall

taking a front seat to the show.

Tyra undresses Sunny and trails kisses

along her neck, breast, belly and thighs. "May I

have some of MY yummy, Sunny? I've missed

her." Tyra says seductively. Sunny whispers a

yes as she opens her pussy lips with her hands inviting Tyra inside. Sunny was already dripping wet. "You have the most beautiful clit, Sun. I want you to cum hard for me. I need you to cum all over my face. Understood?"

Sunny is quivering, anticipating Tyra's tongue on her clit. She isn't thinking about Ahmaad, Ezra, her baby... anything. She just wants to feel good. She wants to escape into the land of Euphoria. "Understood" Sunny moans. Tyra encircles Sunny's clit slowly. Making the head protrude. She then makes the number 8 with her tongue over and over again until Sunny's clit starts to pulsate. Tyra sucks on Sunny's clit then switches to figure 8's then sucks then 8's over and over until Sunny's clit is rock hard, ready to release the floodgates of her soul.

Sunny looks over at Joanie and she is finger fucking herself: enjoying every minute of her girlfriend devouring Sunny's pussy. Sunny can't hold on; she lets go and squirts into Tyra's mouth like a geyser. "Oh shiiittttt!!" Sunny screams out. Tyra begins tongue fucking Sunny. She wants everything Sunny has to give. "Sunny you're so fucking sweet. Oh my god, give me more Sunny!" Sunny couldn't take anymore. She fell off the couch because her clit was too sensitive to take another lick. "You ok Sunny? Don't you run from this tongue." They all laugh out loud. "Oh my God bitch. I forgot how amazing you are with your mouth. Don't make me fall in love with you too." Sunny and Joanie laughed but Tyra didn't find the humor.

Probably because she secretly was in love with her best friend. "The towels are in the hall closet. Go help yourself to a shower before you go home to your new boyfriend, bitch." Tyra tells Sunny. Sunny tries to wash all of her worries away in the shower. "Why do I always turn to sex for an escape? What is wrong with me? I can't keep this shit up." Sunny thought to herself. She always wondered if being molested as a child turned her into the girl who seeks comfort with sex.

"Thanks for everything T. I'll see you sooner than later. Nice to meet you Joanie." Joanie bids Sunny a farewell. "Just because I ate your pussy doesn't mean you need to get ghost for another 3 months on me. Don't act funny bitch." Tyra scolds Sunny. "Okay damnnn! I love you T." Sunny walks outside to find all four of her tires slashed and every window shattered. The words *"slut bitch"* was carved on the hood of the car. "Oh my fucking goodness. This is only the beginning."

Sunny says as she drops her purse. She turns around to head back up to Tyra's apartment. She sees Ezra running towards her out the corner of her eye. She runs as fast as she could up the stairs, yelling for Tyra to open the door. Tyra opened the door just in time. "Call 911!" Sunny yells at Tyra.

Sunny makes a police report and presses charges against Ezra. She calls Ahmaad and he comes to her aide right away. He gets her car towed to a shop he knows and takes care of all repairs. "Sunny fuck that weak nigga. I got you...I got yall. Everything will be ok. You just keep that paperwork going on his ass just in case I have to do something permanent." Sunny is exhausted and speechless. Ahmaad takes her home.

"We don't have to talk right now but we need to eventually about last night Sunny. Just get some rest for now." Sunny shakes her head and sleeps for 10 hours straight. She wakes up looking for Ahmaad. She hears him in his spare room. She opens the door and she sees Babies "R" Us bags everywhere. "Baby what did you do?" Sunny says with tears in her eyes. "I got little man right. I just wanted to take some things off your mind Sun. We got to get prepared. He will be here in 4 months bae." Ahmaad says proudly.

"Baby I...I....thank you Ahmaad. Thank you for being my angel." Sunny is sobbing. She looks around and sees diapers, wipes, dozens upon dozens of baby boy clothes, a bassinet, bottles, a bouncy seat and changing table. Ahmaad means exactly what Ahmaad says. Despite all of the chaos, Sunny feels she made the right decision choosing Ahmaad.

Sunny is full term and is due to deliver any day now. She and Ahmaad seem like a married couple. She couldn't be happier. His family has even embraced her and bought things for the baby. She doesn't want or need for anything. Ezra hasn't contacted her since he spent 30 days in jail after destroying her car and chasing her. She finished another semester of school and things couldn't be better. She felt the need to clean incessantly. She has the music blasting and is cleaning the house top to bottom while Ahmaad is at work. While washing the windows she heard a splat on the hardwood floor. Her water broke. "Oh shit! Oh my god what do I do? Ok calm down Sun. Let's call Ahmaad. Ahmaad umm I think my water broke." Sunny tells Ahmaad. "What? Ok bae I'm on my way. Just sit down. Get a towel and put it in between your legs. I'm coming." Ahmaad flew home. By the time he got to Sunny she was doubled over on the floor screaming in pain.

"Ahmaad help me!!! I feel something in my pussy. Help! Call 911!" Sunny is yelling at the top of her lungs in pain. Ahmaad dials 911. "Hello, 911 fire or medical emergency?" "Um hello my wife is having a baby I think. She says she feels something in her vagina and we are home." Ahmaad is shaking with fear. The 911 operator tells him exactly what to do. He gets towels and blankets and tells Sunny to lie down. "I can't fucking lie down. I can't' fucking do it. Help me now!!" Sunny is on all fours and screaming her lungs out. Ahmaad looks at her vagina and sees the baby's head. "Lady the baby head is out! Help me!" "Ok sir calm down.

Tell your wife to breathe and let her body push the baby out. But you have to catch it ok! Sir?" Ahmaad is a nervous wreck. "It's out! It's out! I mean he is out! I got him!" The baby and Ahmaad are crying. "Hi little man. We've been waiting on you." Ahmaad says. "Sir, the paramedics are at your door. Let them in and congratulations!" The 911 operator says.

"Thank you!" Ahmaad tells the operator. "Here baby, meet your son." Ahmaad passes the baby to Sunny and rushes to the door. Sunny falls deeply in love with her son. It was love at first sight. As soon as she laid him on her chest he stopped crying. Sunny started crying. It was a beautiful unforgettable moment.

At the hospital Ahmaad calls Sunny's family about the news. No one knew who he was because Sunny cut all contact. But her entire family came to the hospital bearing gifts. Word got out to Ezra that his son was born. He texted Sunny and asked to see his son. "Maad what do I do?" Sunny asks Ahmaad. "Send him a picture. Tell him he will get notice of paternity test and we will move forward from there. He fucked up Sun. He could've seen him but he

took that away when he did what he did to you."
Sunny does what Ahmaad says and sends him
the text. Ezra doesn't respond.

The coming weeks are filled with sleepless
nights and breast feeding but Sunny couldn't be
happier. Ahmaad was with her every step of the
way as if this baby was his flesh and blood. As
far as Sunny was concerned Ahmaad was
Caleb's father. "Sunny the test results came
today." Ahmaad yells out after getting the mail.
Sunny opens the results and of course they read
99.9% Ezra Carmichael is the father. "I wonder
what this fool will do now." Sunny says under
her breath. "That fool better go to court. That's
what. Baby I gotta go make this money. I will
be back before 10:00 tonight okay? Gimme kiss
mama. Love you. Daddy love you too Caleb."

Ahmaad plants kisses on baby Caleb's little head. Sunny loved Ahmaad more and more every day. She still has a hard time believing how good he is to her and Caleb. She is amazed. Sunny dozes off with baby Caleb on her chest.

She wakes up to her phones notifications going off. It's Ezra sending her dozens of pictures. It's Ahmaad with the girl he kicked out of his house a few months back when Sunny popped up. They're outside his car talking and laughing. He is leaning in close to her but nothing else from the pictures. The last text message says karma.

Sunny drops her phone and she sees stars and hears ringing. She is confused. Not sure what's happening to her. She sees someone picking up her baby. It's Ezra. He broke into their house and hit her in the back of the head with the butt of his gun. "My son belongs at home with me." Ezra says. "Give me my fucking baby you sick bastard!" Sunny tries to get up and charge Ezra. But she's stopped in her tracks. All she hears is ringing and she feels blood pouring from her mouth and chest.

Ezra shot sunny. He shot her in cold blood. Sunny collapses to the ground and tries to scream Caleb, but only a faint whisper comes out. She sees Caleb in Ezra's arms as he walks out of the door and leaves her to die alone. As Sunny lay drowning in her own blood she sees glimpses of her life, and wonder "how did I end up here. God please don't let me die, if you give me one more chance I promise to live my life the way you see fit. Just give me another chance

God I'm not ready to leave my child. Please don't let me leave I have to make it up to my baby."

Ahmaad comes home and finds Sunny unconscious covered in her blood. He is hysterical. Ahmaad calls 911, "My girlfriend is bleeding and she isn't awake. I don't know what's going on please send someone now!" The 911 operator asks Ahmaad to try and locate the source from which she is bleeding and apply pressure. Sunny is grayish blue and her breathing is very faint.

"Baby please hold on. Please don't leave me. Don't leave me baby we need you here. Where is the baby Sunny?" Ahmaad doesn't let Sunny go but he is looking around frantically for the baby. Where is Caleb Sunny?" Sunny is slipping away.

Ahmaad knows exactly what has happened now. Paramedics come and whisk Sunny away to Beaumont hospital. Ahmaad calls Sunny's parents and heads straight to Ezra's, fully armored.

"I'm going to kill this muthafucka!"